HALL
- LORE -
WEEN

JOSH SPERO
WITH SPECIAL GUEST
K.J. DAVIS

Castling
Books

Castling Books

An Imprint of CASTLE BRIDGE MEDIA
Denver, Colorado

Edited by Jason Henderson & In Churl Yo
Stories by Josh Spero
Special Guest Author K.J. Davis
Editing by Leigh Fryling
Interior Art by TT Hernandez
Cover Art by Aldo Avelar
Book Design by Brett Jasper

This book is a work of fiction. Names, characters, business, events, and incidents are the products of the author's imagination. Any resemblance to actual persons, living or dead or actual events is purely coincidental.

HALL-LORE-WEEN
©2024 Josh Spero
All rights reserved.

ISBN: 979-8-9895934-7-7

No part of this book may be reproduced, stored in a retrieval system, or transmitted in any form or by any means, electronic, mechanical, photocopying, recording, or otherwise, without the prior written permission of the author, except as provided by U.S.A. copyright law.

ACKNOWLEDGEMENTS

This book is dedicated to
My mother, Harriet Spero. RIP mom.
My late uncle, Mike Bushler. He's responsible
for my Halloween obsession.

Special Dedication
To my lovely wife, Robin Spero. If not for her, many of these
stories would not be possible. She is my muse, my love, my life.
We did it, Babe.

NOTE FROM THE AUTHOR

Dear Reader,

Have you ever felt a little different from those that surround you? Have you been more intrigued by the dark than the light? Do you lean more towards the spooky side of life than the wholesome or sweet? You are not alone. This voice calling me to the darkness is what drove me to write this book. Where most people feel scared and vulnerable when the lights go out, I find a sense of comfort and belonging. If you feel as I do, let this book be a call to arms. Let this book allow you to release your inner monster and plug into these worlds. The horror community has always had to survive submissive to mainstream pop culture. By supporting the horror community, we can build it up and bring it to the masses. We can make the horror genre as popular as sports. I mean, why not? It offers us entertainment and a method to escape the confines of our daily lives, much like sports do. Except that when the sporting event ends, the horror story can stay with us, haunting us for the rest of our lives. My hope is that this book will be a new staple in this wonderful macabre culture. I hope you dust it off each Halloween season and revisit the little stories within. Share them with your family and friends. But, above all, spread the love of horror. Please enjoy.

Your horror companion,

Josh Spero

NOTE FROM THE EDITOR

As a former spooky kid who became a spooky grown-up who now HAS a spooky kid, I'm happy to be a part of a book that we can read together. Keep being yourself, keep reading what you love, and stay spooky!

Leigh Fryling

CONTENTS

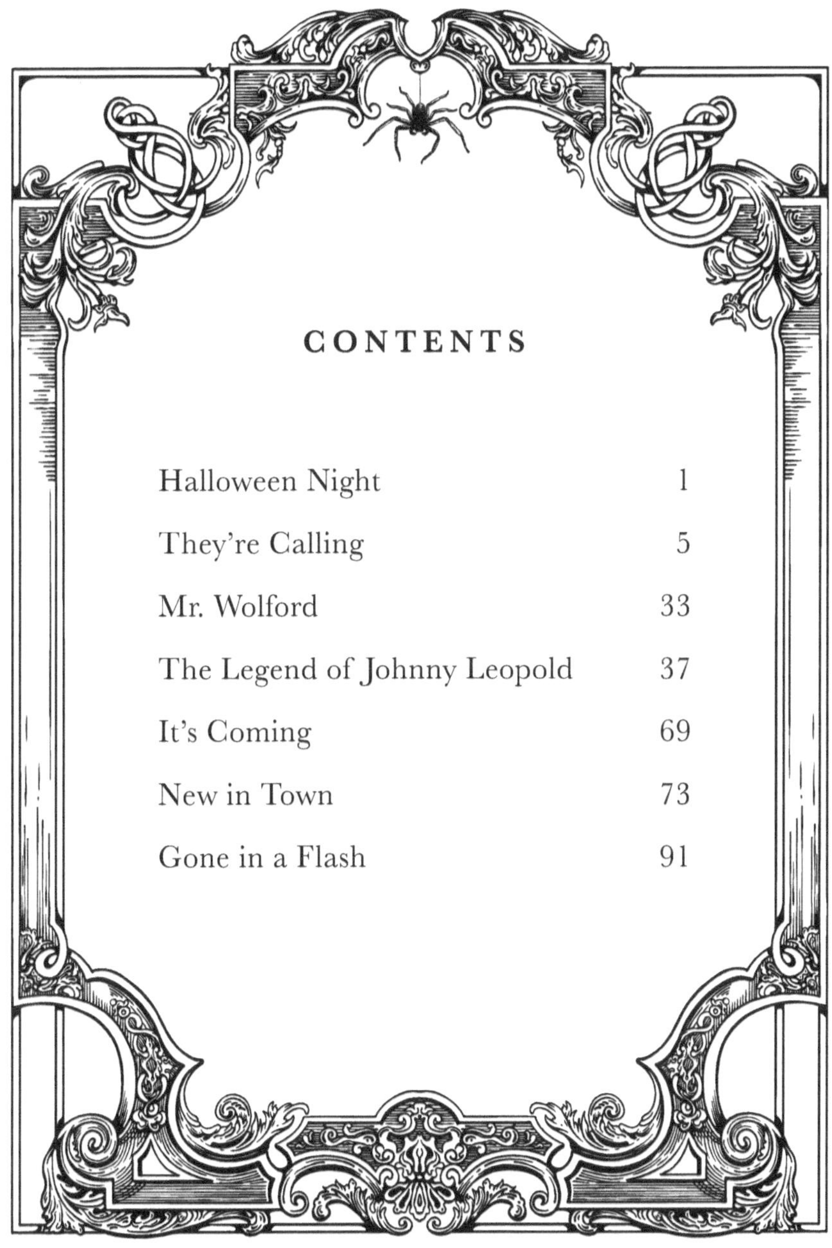

Halloween Night	1
They're Calling	5
Mr. Wolford	33
The Legend of Johnny Leopold	37
It's Coming	69
New in Town	73
Gone in a Flash	91

PREFACE

Hello, my creepy friends,

It's me, Jacko, the three-eyed Jack-o-lantern.

I'm bringing you some Halloween goodies that I conjured up for this year's spooky season. The stories and poems within these pages are scary tales of some friends of mine that live very unusual lives. I hope they are not too frightening for you—but no promises! All of them are related to the season of frights and delights. So whether you are diving into these stories for the first time or revisiting them as a Halloween tradition, you're about to embark on a trip into the land of the dark.

Welcome to Hall-Lore-Ween…

Jacko

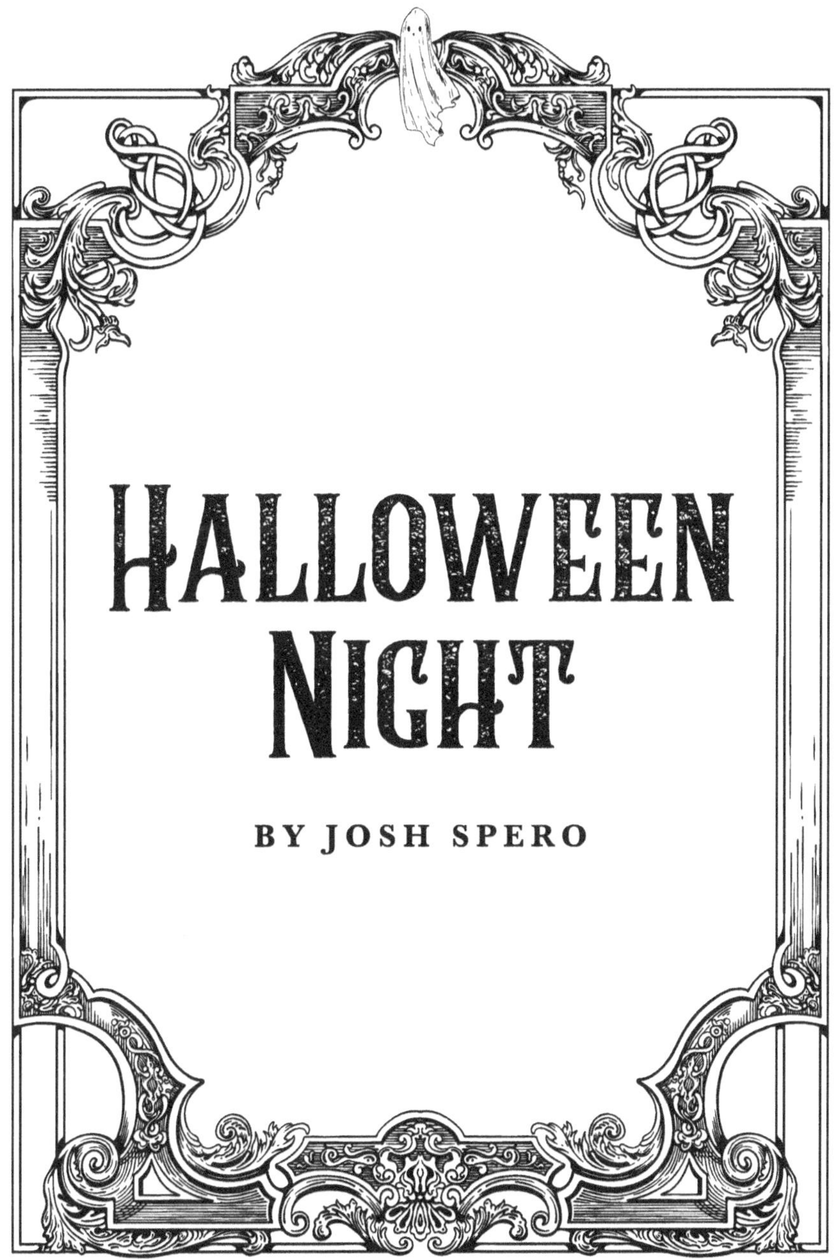

HALLOWEEN NIGHT

BY JOSH SPERO

And now, another Halloween
That's surely bound to make you scream.
With goblins, ghouls, and scary creatures;
Monsters with such ghastly features.

Wolves that howl and sound real mean,
And ghosts that shriek but can't be seen.
Skeletons dancing through the streets,
Next to kids who wear bed-sheets.

On this night it's trick or treat,
And for best costume all compete.
With jack-o-lanterns glowing bright,
And witches' spells that cause real fright.

The paths are lit by candlelight,
And lead to things that don't seem right.
Now how can we forget the candy?
That's why pillowcases come in handy.

Making this a night of fun,
But now the stitches come undone.
All the costumes fall to the ground,
You stop and take a look around.

All the kids you thought were there,
Are gone—and now the streets are bare.
You realize that they never were,
And now your mind begins to stir.

They're all just spirits out to scare,
This all must be some daft nightmare.
Wake up! It's still Halloween morning,
But consider this your only warning.

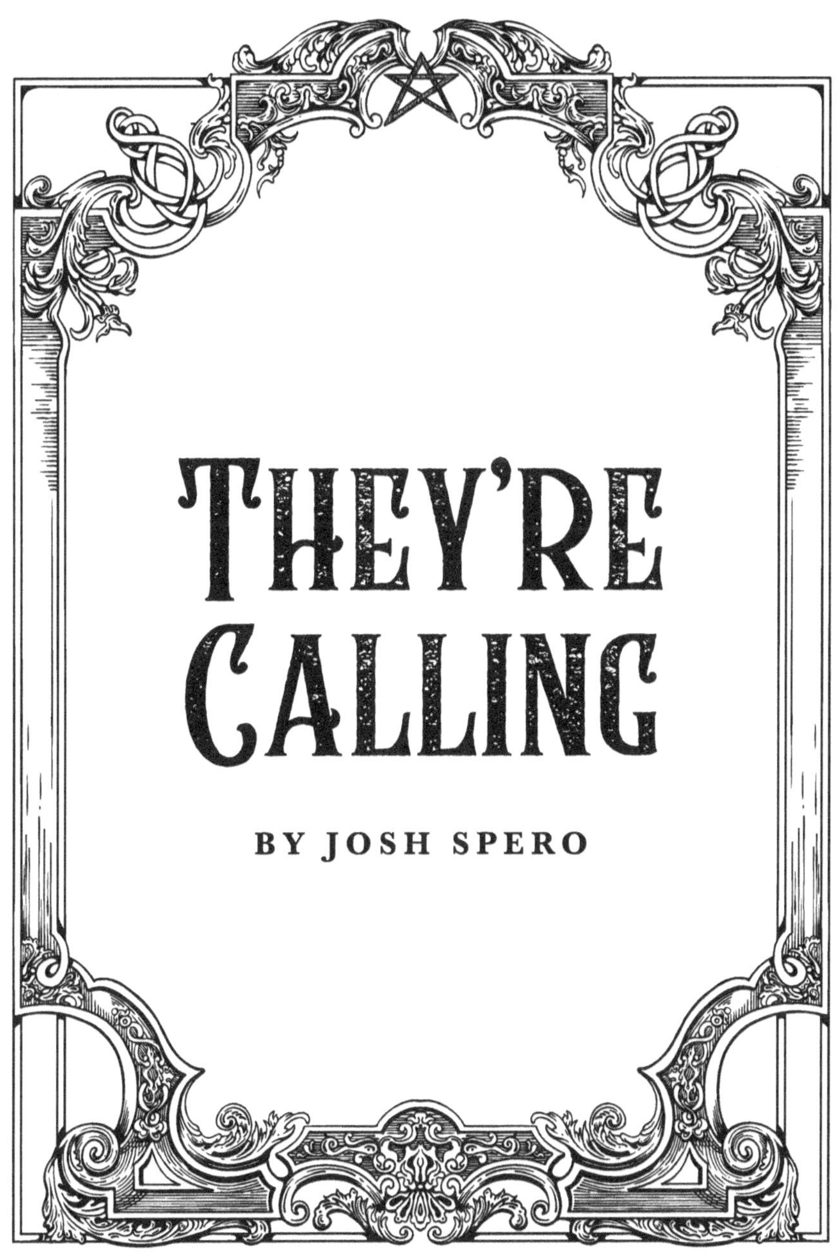

THEY'RE CALLING

BY JOSH SPERO

The monotonous flashing of road reflectors sparkled in her eyes, sending Cynnie Parker into a mindless trance. She had been driving for eight hours on a solo mission, with only twenty-five miles left to go. Her eyes grew heavy, her head started to bob in synch with the rough patches in the blacktop. She sprang to life at the loud hum of tires caressing the rumble strips with a gasp and a flutter in her chest. Where was she? She couldn't remember the last road sign, the last turn-off…or even getting into the car. Looking around, utterly confused, her mind raced to put the pieces together. "*Why am I here? What is going on?*" She knew it made for bad driving, but she grabbed for her phone and played back her last recorded voice memo.

This was her coping mechanism, the voice memos, circumventing her random spells of temporary short-term memory lapse. They were rare, thank goodness. She had, as the doctors suggested she might, grown out of them for the most part. As time passed, so did the blackouts.

Of course, until right now.

A recording of her own voice explained everything she needed to return her memory, and breath returned to her lungs. *Right right right.* Aunt is dead, almost there, everything is fine. Now, slightly more awake, she increased the volume on the eighty's playlist blaring from the car speakers. Singing along, her concentration was broken when the music turned to static. *What the heck is happening?* she thought. *How can there be static with my phone plugged in?* Suddenly, through the static, a voice started whispering. A mutter that she could not understand came through the speakers. She punched a few buttons on the touch screen—maybe—the Bluetooth had cut out and she was picking up radio channel. She waited, ignoring it, hoping the tech would kick back in.

One voice quickly became two different distinct voices, then three. It didn't sound like radio...maybe it was cell interference. She reached out to turn off the radio. Quiet would be fine until she could get back into some kind of cell range. The car clicked into silence, and she shook her head.

WRRIEEET.

She shrieked in fear and shock as the voices came back. The sound crescendoed, and as it did, the greater her skin crawled.

"STOP IT," she screamed.

Instantly the volume and song returned to the previous playlist. She pulled over on the side of the road for a moment just to regain her composure. She rested her forehead on the steering wheel.

"Silver lining," she muttered. "At least this stupid thing is a rental."

She checked the phone's navigation to see if she was still on track. Thirty minutes out. She smacked her hand against the side of the steering wheel.

"Come on, Cynnie!" she shouted out loud, staring at herself in the rearview mirror. "Thirty more measly minutes, then we're there. Don't lose it now!" She ran her fingers through her hair and massaged her temples. After taking a long, hard look at herself, she noticed that yesterday's makeup had worn off her forehead, revealing a scar over her left eye. She chimed in again, "Thank goodness nobody is in this car. You look torn up, girl!" Her self-deprecation was interrupted by a flashing sign behind her reflection in the rear view. ROSIE'S ROADSIDE: BREAKFAST SERVED ALL DAY. Pancakes at two am? *Best idea in the world right now*, her stomach said. Coffee wouldn't be a bad idea either. She popped the car into reverse and made a little backwards path to a parking spot.

Cynnie made it to the entrance of the diner without her feet touching the floor. The sign in the lobby stated PLEASE SEAT YOURSELF, so she plopped down in an open booth and scooped a menu out of the condiment/menu display. It was slightly greasy to the touch—something —her dad would have said was a good sign. *If the spoon is greasy, you're gonna be happy*, he'd say.

She jumped again as a cheerful voice snapped her out of her reverie.

"Hey there. What can I get started for ya, darlin'?" a loud, twangy voice billowed from behind the menu. A plump and smiling older waitress stood in a pink outfit right off the set of *Happy Days*. A plastic name tag read PEGGY.

Cynnie dropped the menu as though it had been set on fire.

"Criminy! Sorry hun, I didn't mean ta scare ya. Can I get your order?"

Cynnie let out the breath she'd been holding with a strangled chuckle. "Coffee, coffee, and more coffee, please. And two pancakes," she said, when her heartbeat had settled.

"Sure! Be back in a jiffy."

And a jiffy it was. Cynnie barely had time to register that there were a few other patrons nursing coffee or pouring honey on grits, or where the bathrooms were before Peggy was back with a mug and a small pot that she poured generously from.

"Where you from little stranger? We don't have eyes that pretty color green around here, you must be from up North."

"Oh, well, thank you. I come from a little town called Temecula. It's in California."

"California, huh?" Peggy exclaimed. "Well, it's a pleasure to make your acquaintance. Hope you enjoy your visit—what — brings you all the way out here from California?"

"Well, I used to live around here when I was much younger, but my mother and I moved around so much back then that I don't really remember much about the area. Unfortunately, my aunt Millie——Mildred—passed away, leaving me her property. It's only a few miles from here. So, that's where I'm headed."

"Wow. Are you gonna sell it, or become a new local?

"Honestly, I was thinking of sticking around for a while. I really need a change in my life. I was a nurse back in California, and those long twelve-hour shifts were eating me up, you know?"

Peggy snorted, then threw a knowing glance at the other customers, as if to say *I can relate*.

"I'm hoping to slow things down and start being present in

my own life, if you know what I mean."

"I sure do. Well, I've been living 'round these parts for over forty years. So, if you need a tour guide I only cost forty dollars per hour." Peggy said with a motherly wink. "Where is your new property? I know every inch of this area within fifty miles."

"You know? I'm not too sure. It's about five miles from here I guess. Somewhere off Abbots Way. I guess the place is called Umbra Den?"

The entire restaurant paused at once, and people turned to stare. The eerie silence drew her attention to the realization that she was alone.

"Why is everyone staring at me?" Cynnie whispered to Peggy. The warm and welcoming smile melted off of Peggy's face like soft wax under a flame as she grabbed the cross around her neck and kissed it.

"Oh, my word. Darlin', you can't go there. It's not safe for you. That is an evil and... *unholy* place. You said your *aunt* lived there?"

Taken aback, Cynnie nodded. "Well, yes. I never got to actually meet her. She and my mom had a huge falling out before I was born. They never spoke again, and I lost my mom when I was ten years old. I never had the opportunity to meet my aunt. I didn't even know she was still alive until the lawyer called me. I was her only kin; that's why I'm the new owner. Um... Should I be concerned? Is there a real threat?" she asked as the people began to return to their meals already in progress.

"Let's just say that nobody travels out that way. I mean *nobody*.

I suppose if the place is vacant now, you might be okay. Normally I wouldn't say boo about anybody's business… but please, be strong in your faith, whatever that may be. I will pray for you, girl."

Cynnie finished her meal. What had been a carefree vacation at six that morning had turned into a strange dark quest into the unknown. She walked to the counter to pay, squirming a little under the low gazes of the diners.

"Honey, I'm gonna give you two numbers." Peggy scribbled and pointed at the first of two phone numbers. "This one here is mine. This one *here*, that's Mother Abernathy over at the convent in Sohoma. You need anything…well, you just call."

"Thanks, Peggy."

"Say your prayers, girl. I'll be sayin' mine."

She took the little piece of receipt paper. Now, a little reluctant to go, Cynnie forced herself to turn to the door. After all, it was too late to turn back now. Or rather, too early in the morning.

She pulled up to the house shortly after leaving the dinner. The dark was so complete out here that she could only see what was before the car's headlights. What they revealed was not a comfort. After dreaming about a soft bed and a good rest, she wanted to cry after seeing how eerie and run-down the place looked. Frankly, too much like a crummy cabin from an old horror movie.

Bad enough not to sleep in.

It was about 3:30 a.m. She decided to sleep in her car with a blanket over her head and the car locked up tight. I've seen way too many movies. I'll investigate in the morning with daylight on my side. Plus, with that raving review from the townsfolk, I choose to live.

Luckily, the sunlight didn't come crashing through the car windows until about 9:30 a.m. The thick foliage surrounding the property left her enough darkness to sleep a little longer. Slowly coming to, she rummaged a granola bar and a bottle of water out of her purse and made a breakfast of it. A far cry from Peggy's pancakes. But, after the snack and the sleep, it wasn't long before her curiosity drove her to explore further.

Little beams of light cracked through the thick foliage that lay just beyond a decomposing wood shanty, spotlighting areas of the long neglected homestead. Relics of the past lay scattered throughout the landscape; an old hand—powered washing machine, half a flour barrel, a sad old leather book sprouting black—eyed Susans. Just past the tall, dead grass that covered the yard lay what you could loosely call a house. Abundant vines embraced the facade, nearly camouflaging the cabin. What little areas of the exposed wooden skeleton that crept through the vines told a tale of decades passed.

As she approached, the scent of old musty wood grew stronger. The steps creaked and shifted under her feet, causing her to lose her balance. She reached for the handrail, only to find out that half of it was missing. With a large thud, she sprawled out across the porch. Nothing was wounded but her pride, and she tried to chuckle. *Thank goodness nobody was around to see that.*

The front door was slightly open, which gave her a moment's pause. She decided to proceed and entered the house with extreme caution but could not have prepared herself for what lay within.

A veil of dust coated everything and spread throughout the

air, which was only visible in the rays of light intruding through the broken window panes. The floors were worn planks of wood like a ghost town's boardwalk. The walls were paved with large stones that were encased with cobwebs. There was an over-sized fireplace with a large wooden plank mantle. In the fireplace was a cauldron on a mount with strange grooves in the metal. *They look like scratches,* she thought, before shaking the idea away.

There were several dilapidated bookshelves, some with antique books, but most were lined with little apothecary bottles. Many of the labels were either too worn out to read or had strange symbols on them. But something else was…strange? Wrong? There was electricity; she had passed an ancient light switch on the way in. But there were no light fixtures. Instead, there were candles and oil lamps everywhere. *What is this, a witch's house? Nibble nibble, like a mouse…*

The most startling discovery, however, hung over her head. Above the fireplace was a large, painted portrait of her aunt Mildred. She was pretty in an unsettling sort of way. Eyes slightly too far apart. Cheekbones just a little too low to be aristocratic. Her head was slightly tilted forward, as though she were about to laugh.

Cynnie took a quick step back from the painting. There was nothing else in the frame, just her aunt's face. The black background wasn't quite perfect however—the variations in tone made it seem like there was someone standing there behind Mildred. Creepy.

She took a few moments to fixate upon the painting, as this was the first time she had really seen her aunt. There was definitely a strong family resemblance. She saw a lot of her mother in her aunt, which made the creep factor slightly less severe. But it still felt like she was eavesdropping on some past conversation she shouldn't be hearing. *What the heck did I get myself into now? Did we have a witch in the family? Is this why Mom stopped talking to you?*

Eventually she shook off the spell of the portrait. If she was going to deal with… this, —whatever it was, she was going to need to see if it was even possible to stay on the property. She poked around the little cabin. Really the outside was the worst of it—the —the interior was quite charming in a hermitage kind of way. Luckily, there was a refrigerator and plumbing that worked. Promising start. The ancient brass bed was comfy enough, though it desperately needed new linens. All in all, (and as she had suspected) it wasn't so bad in daylight. *One quick trip through a Megamart and this place could be cozy.* Done, then. She would make the best of the situation and find a way to settle in.

Megamart there was not—but —the little town of Abbotsford was surprisingly well provisioned. Between the Baptist Church Charity Shop, a small grocery store, and a Dollar General which the townsfolk referred to as "the BuckStop," Cynnie soon had everything she needed for a prolonged stay.

As time passed, the quaint town took on a slow southern charm that seemed oddly familiar. Though she still caught the odd sideways glance from people, she was becoming more comfortable. She went on long daily rambles through the town to get more acquainted with all the local businesses and townsfolk. It wasn't difficult for her to be social in this friendly little place.

One Wednesday morning, Cynnie was shopping at the

Hilliard Grocery Store in the center of town. Aisle by aisle she scoured through shelves for essentials. She hummed along to an old Talking Heads tune playing through the speakers. *Run run run run run run run away…ooooooohhh…*

Unexpectedly, the music tapered off into silence in the middle of the song. She glanced up, feeling disquieted. She flashed back briefly to the strange problem with the radio in the car.

So when something whispered directly behind her, so softly that it was incomprehensible, she jumped. Startled, Cynnie spun around—and found nobody there. The entire aisle was empty.

The whispers didn't stop. She walked over to the next aisle to see if the voice came through the shelves. Empty. She searched each of the other aisles to find the entire store empty. There had been at least twenty people in the store when she arrived, but now it looked abandoned. She heard another whisper—only this time it was accompanied by another. *It's happening again,* she thought as panic grew. As the voices grew louder, she closed her eyes, covered her ears, and screamed. Not a moment later, she opened her eyes to find an older couple standing cart-to-cart in front of her.

"My goodness, are you all right?" the old man asked.

She looked around to realize there were several people staring at her. "Uh, I'm okay. I'm so sorry. I am okay. I just thought I saw a bug. Really big one. Please excuse me," she muttered, grabbing her cart and speeding away.

Still disoriented, she took a corner and collided with a man pushing a stock cart. Cans of green beans and corn went sprawling across the floor in every direction. So did her feet. In the commotion, she stepped on a can and gravity did the rest. The falling sensation was slow, almost dreamlike—until she was stopped abruptly by a pair of arms.

"I got you, ma'am!"

The man's blue apron matched his eyes. That was about all she could register between the adrenaline of the scare, the fall, and the catch. He helped her up, and they both took stock of the wreckage before they turned toward each other.

"I am *so* sorry. Are you okay?" he asked, somewhere between amusement and panic.

"I am now!" she said, staring at him for a moment before she realized how that sounded. "Because you caught me, I mean! Not like, umm.."

"Excuse me?" he said, clearly confused.

"I meant, thank you for grabbing me, ah… I mean catching, with your arms, which are nice. WAS nice. Nice arms. Good catch! Ah—" *Shut up, Cynnie. Get yourself out of this situation, now!* She could feel the tips of her ears turning red with embarrassment as the flush crawled up her face. *In for a penny…*

"I'm sorry. I have to go die now." Without waiting for a response, she grabbed her cart and sped off down the last aisle. *Idiot. All you had to say was thank you. Thank you pretty—nice, pretty nice man. Arms. What is wrong with me!?*

Within five minutes post-collision, she finished her shopping and quickly trotted to the checkout stand. Those same blue eyes started tracking her from behind the register. Her trot crept down to a crawl.

"Well, I'm glad you're not dead yet." He said with a gentle smirk, inviting her to join in the joke.

Perfect. Just my luck, she thought while trying desperately not to make eye contact. As she approached she blurted out, "Aren't you the stock boy? Guy? Man? Stock-man?"

Stock-man threw his hands up and shrugged, "Oh, it's worse than that. I own this grocery store."

Cynnie could feel the color draining from her face. *The owner.*

"Look, I'm not normally a klutz. I was just startled, that's all." Cynnie began to explain in a panic.

"Completely understood. Absolutely no judgment, ma'am."

"Cynnie! The name's Cynnie."

"Well, it's a pleasure to make your acquaintance, Cynnie. I've never met a Cynnie before."

"It's short for Cynthia, but I've been called Cynnie since I was in diapers. Cynnie Parker, at your service!" she said with a smile and a mock salute.

"Well, Cynnie Parker. My name is Brock, but people just call me Brock." He said with a wink. "Are you new around here? I haven't seen you before."

"Yes, I am. Just got a place on the edge of town."

"Nice! Well, welcome to town. I'm definitely looking forward to seeing you around here more often." Brock said while he continued to place her groceries into a brown paper bag. After the last item, he placed an orange flier into the bag that caught her eye.

"What's that for?" She asked.

"Oh, it's a flier for the Town Halloween Bash on Saturday. You should come. It'll be a great way to meet new people and see the town. The parade begins at 6:30 p.m. in Town Square. Costume contest at eight. It's kind of a big deal around here." Brock said.

Delighted at the quaintness of an old town putting on a Halloween parade, she couldn't resist the large smile that ran across her face.

"Maybe I'll see you there?" Brock asked.

"Maybe you will. We'll see." She tossed a smile back his way as she exited the store.

That's only three days from now, she thought. I'll buy a witch's hat and some makeup. Maybe some old jewelry. I'm sure Auntie Mildred has something lying around that should fit the bill.

Her plan could not have gone any better. As soon as she returned to the house, she opened a side closet in the master bedroom. There were several long robes and cloaks, one for each of the primary fall colors. Several of them had sigils and insignias embroidered into them.

"Wow. These are…"

Suddenly, the little cabin made a little more sense. If the townspeople threw a big Halloween bash every year, maybe Aunt Mildred was a part of it? That would explain a lot. Cauldron, spooky cabin exterior, these amazing cloaks…Yeah. That made a lot more sense.

More sense than what? Aunt Mildred being a witch?

Cynnie spent two hours getting ready on the night of the parade. *You gotta look convincingly evil, but still cute in case you see Brock.*

Wicked but cute. Wicked cute! HA! She glanced in the bathroom mirror. The spiderweb eye makeup was a nice touch she thought. And the glow in the dark nail polish was definitely going to be a hit when it got dark. On her way out the door, she glanced back at the cabin. Her heart skipped a beat. Something was different. Wasn't it? She looked at the portrait, narrowing her eyes in focus. Was it the portrait?

But Mildred looked as unsettling and alluring as ever. The ghostly presence in the black background was still there. The chill that went down her spine wasn't from the open door, but she shook it off anyway. Things always looked a little creepier on Halloween.

Placing her hat firmly on her head, she descended upon the town, broom in hand. There was a cool breeze in the air on her walk. Several other families accompanied her on her way, and the joy they exuded engulfed her. With each step she took toward the event, her excitement grew, and the moving herd grew with it. She hadn't even arrived at the town's center yet and she had already seen monsters, robots, little bumble bees, the entire entourage from *The Wizard of Oz,* and so much more. Each street that she passed was veiled with décor and lights in a manner that she had never experienced. She was truly amazed at the level of effort that the small town went through to execute this level of celebration.

When she finally did get to Town Center, she was floored by the sight. It looked like an elaborate dark carnival with games, food booths, and a large stage draped with dozens of Jack-o-lanterns on a sprawling community lawn. All fifteen-hundred residents must have been there with more from the surrounding towns. *Big deal indeed,* she thought.

The only disappointment in her evening was no sign of Brock the Stockman. Oh well. The people-watching was entertainment in and of itself. Watching kids race around in their myriad of costumes, bemused parents in tow, spying awkward teens holding court between the carnival stalls. It was almost overwhelmingly fun. Was this what she had been missing, working those wild hours as a nurse? Never seeing the light of day, no time for community, for escape? She sat down on a hay bale and looked around. *This could be my life. This right here. I wonder how crazy they go for Christmas!*

Lost in thought, she didn't notice the whispers until they were almost a roar, the maddening sounds blending in with the hum of the crowd. The senseless noise grew, crashed, crescendoed in her ears, her mind, her pounding heart. Her eyes bounced around frantically, desperate to locate the source, starting to water with the pressure of the noise. She clapped her hands over her ears, groaning in pain, and threw her head down. The world spun. She thought she was going to throw up.

Everything stopped.

The relief she felt at the silence was short lived. She looked up to see a tall, austere woman, clad in a similar cloak to Cynnie's, staring at her with blind, milky eyes. Everything else, every*one* else, was frozen. Cynnie leapt to her feet, alarm bells replacing the whispers in her head. Spinning around, she spotted three other figures in similar attire, also staring at her with mannequinesque stillness. By the time she turned back, the first woman had gotten so close that Cynnie could feel her warm, fetid breath on her face.

"Mildred? Did you stop answering your sisters? Are you turning your back on your coven? Have you gone *rogue?*"

The screechy, aggressive voice sped toward her, growing like a Doppler effect into her ears. In barely a blink, another woman joined the blind one, a mature woman with dark, gothic beauty. Her perfume at this distance was mesmerizing, a whirl of vanilla, sweet fruits, and campfire. She had long hair that was black as death, pale white skin, and piercing honey-yellow eyes that raked over Cynnie with confusion and disdain.

Completely flustered, Cynnie said, "I am so sorry. You've made a mistake. I'm not Mildred. I'm her niece, Cynnie. Mildred—I'm so sorry. She just passed away three weeks ago. I'm sorry to break the news to you if you didn't already know. Also, you just—everyone is—how did you—"

The woman turned towards the other three, and Cynnie registered with some panic that she was practically surrounded.

"This is the child. We have found her." She then turned back to Cynnie. "We are sorry for your loss. She has returned to the earth. Child, to which coven do you belong?"

"Who, me? Oh, I am not a witch, this is just a costume."

"Oh, but you *are*. Yes? We can *sense* it, can't we, sisters? You carry the blood. We have been *hunting* you. Haven't you heard us calling? If you have heard our voices in your head then it is *you* that must complete our circle in her stead. It is your responsibility to join us."

"*Join* you?"

The blind woman nodded slowly, and a small, plump woman

took her elbow. "Yes, Child. Auma never makes mistakes. You must join us."

"Join you to do…what?"

The third woman, who looked like she had bitten into a sour apple, offered what Cynnie thought was supposed to be a smile. "Our circle. Our coven. Our family."

"That sounds…nice. But I don't have the faintest idea what that even means. And aren't witches…I don't mean to be rude, please don't think that, but…aren't witches supposed to be evil?"

The four older women pealed with genuine laughter. The sound wasn't unpleasant, but in the silence of the frozen crowd, it felt claustrophobic.

"Evil, Cynnie, is relative. Like all natural forces. Are the snakes that eat the mice in the grain bin evil? Are the worms of the earth that eat away our flesh evil? Evil," the dark haired woman chuckled. "We are above such labels."

Cynnie sat back down slowly. "This is… a lot."

The blind woman nodded, perhaps sympathetically.

"Can I… is there time for me to think about it?" Cynnie asked, to relieve the pressure of the encompassing women.

"You have one week to decide. Yes? We will call again. If you decline, a memory spell will be cast. We do not wish to be *known,*" the dark haired leader said sternly. "However, till then, I will give you what has been taken from you."

The witch held up her open palm flat in front of her mouth, whispered a word that Cynnie's mind couldn't find the shape of, and blew. Cynnie's breath was stolen from her as a large cloud of powder consumed her, filling her lungs and burning her eyes. She choked and spluttered for what had to be a full minute before her breath returned. By the time her eyes stopped watering, all that was left of the women were scorched footprints in the scattered hay.

What. Was. That.

Amidst her bewilderment, she heard a voice. "May I hang out with you for a spell?" She turned around to see Brock standing just behind her in a fairly convincing Viking costume. "See what I did there?" he added with a huge, dorky smile.

Too much sugar, that's what it had been. Too much sugar, plus maybe someone had spiked the apple cider. None of that had happened. Because that would be insane. *Oh god, am I going insane?*

"Cynnie?"

She tried to right herself and smiled back. "Was that a re-Thorical question?"

Brock stared for a moment, then roared with laughter. "Funny and nerdy and beautiful. I might have to go full viking and carry you off on a date."

"I promise to pretend I'm resisting, to save your reputation."

They grinned at each other, and in that quick click that sometimes happens between people, knew they were about to have a wonderful time.

The rest of the night was picturesque. Brock was a miserable shot at the beanbag toss but redeemed himself bobbing for apples. Cynnie had the closest guess at the weight of the biggest jack-o-lantern, and won a gift card to the local pub.

"Second date?" said Cynnie, holding up the gift card.

"Third. Unless catching you in the grocery store didn't count."

Brock insisted on walking her home to keep the ghouls and goblins away. Despite the amazing time she was having, the haunting interaction with the coven kept resurfacing in her mind. *A witch? Me? What kind of life would I live? Would I have superpowers?* A million questions flooded her mind on the walk home. She heard something on the periphery of her thoughts, and only realized it had been Brock talking to her when he asked, "So, how does that sound?"

"I'm sorry, say that again?"

"Dinner and drinks, at the pub? Tuesday night? Can I take you out?"

Cynnie smiled. "Yes. I'd like that very much."

They walked up the path toward the cabin. Brock took her hand and slowed their pace. "You know," he said softly. "Seeing you here at the cabin, in the moonlight, I really could believe you are a witch. I'm absolutely under your spell."

He lifted her hand to his lips like an old timey gentleman, and she flushed.

"I…do not have a good comeback for that."

The pair laughed, and the spell was broken. "Goodnight, Brock the Stockman."

"Good night, Cynnie, the Wicked Cute Witch."

They hugged and she ran up the raggedy steps.

By the time she closed the front door, she felt like a Frankenstein—absolutely dead on her feet but pulsing with electricity. She threw her cloak over the peg next to the door, stumbled over to a recliner that sat in the den. Before she knew it she was dead asleep.

The whispers filled the darkness of her dream. She drifted through an empty black space, moving slowly toward the whispers. Into the distance of her black vision walked a figure and a shadow. **Shadow? How can I see a shadow in the dark?** The figure moved closer, walking stiffly, the shadow keeping pace beside it. Something was wrong about the way they moved—the figure too stiff, as though confined by some invisible box, the shadow like a creeping fluid through the darkness.

They were getting faster.

She turned to run, but the slow drift of her movement felt listless and weak. Desperately she tried to focus some kind of energy into moving her dream self, but every time she managed to turn just a little, the figures crept closer. The face. Something was wrong with the face. It was the grey-black blue of the dead and decaying, it was the rotting color of long curdled milk. The thing behind her was dead. The shadow was alive.

The whispers were getting louder and clearer. She could just make out a word:

Cominescori

They were close behind her. She tried to run, to move, anything.

Cominescori

She could see them from the corner of her eye. At any moment they could reach out and grab her.

COMINESCORI

She turned, compelled, commanded.

Mildred's disintegrating head cocked back in a slow grin of triumph, her beauty ruined by three weeks in the grave. Maggots boiled in the holes of her cheeks, and her eyes lay like deflated balloons in their sockets. Cynnie tried to scream, fought for air, but could make no sound.

COMENESCORI

The ghoul of Mildred laughed, a gurgling choke in its gaping throat and pointed a finger at Cynnie's forehead. The shadow wrapped itself like a liquid serpent around the witch's arm, slithered down her forearm, past her finger, moving toward the frozen woman. Cynnie opened her mouth to scream—and the snake-shadow leapt from Mildred's hand, sliding down Cynnie's throat. She could feel its scaled body dragging across the surface of her tongue, catching against the sides of her throat, writhing in her belly—

She woke abruptly, feeling herself choke and gag on air, hot with fear and the struggle for breath. She raced to the tiny bathroom, her stomach roiling in protest. *Too many donuts, that's all this is* said her panicked brain, trying to fight the nausea. She sat there, arms around her knees, fighting for control. Her mind started to drift, her eyes growing heavy again.

The sound of breaking glass snapped her out of the torpor.

She sprang to, clapping a hand over her mouth to keep quiet. The sound continued. She heard a short screech, followed by a soft thump, then a whimper. Whatever it was, it was hurt.

Good. Serve you right, sneaking into my house, whatever you are.

The silence returned, along with the sound of her own breathing. More angry than scared now, she decided to investigate. She slipped off her shoes, padding as quietly as possible in her knee high nylon socks. *I'm coming for you, you—*

Cynnie crept quickly around the corner, and found herself nose-to-nose with a young girl. The mutual scream would have woken dead Aunt Mildred. Before Cynnie could get her bearings, the girl spun on a dime and plunged head first into the banister post that marked the entrance to the stairs. The child collided with such force that she crumpled to the floor and was still.

Anyone else would have panicked at the blood pooling under the girl's head, but deep down, Cynnie was still a nurse. She tended to the wound, placed the girl on the couch, wrapped her in a fleece blanket, and placed an icepack on the goose egg that was forming. Head wounds always bled like crazy, but underneath the red sheen the cut was not bad—not even stitch-worthy, though she may end up with a scar. Cynnie cleaned her up and fixed a butterfly bandage over the spot.

Not five minutes later, the girl opened her eyes and looked around. "Where am I?" she muttered, frightened and confused. A moment later, she was just frightened.

"W-witch!"

"No. No. It's okay. I am not a witch." Cynnie chuckled and wiped a bit of green makeup off her face as proof. "I'm just the lady who lives here. You have nothing to be afraid of. Though you scared the crap out of me—and bumped your noggin on the newel post."

"Me scare you?! *You* scared *me*!" The girl sat up a bit, and hissed through her teeth, touching her forehead gingerly.

"You all right?"

"My head hurts, but I think I'm okay."

"You've got a good size gash there and a bit of a goose egg. I really think we should call the paramedics just to be safe."

"No. It's okay. Honest. Plus, the only doctor near here is Doc Finnegan. He's so old that he don't help nobody much no more."

"Okay, well if not the paramedics, I should probably call the police. Unless you want to tell me why you're out here breaking my windows and your face at midnight on Halloween?"

The girl paled a bit, remembering her entrance. "No, please, don't do that, I'm so sorry, I didn't mean to break your window, it just slammed down so hard after I climbed in and it all broke and I didn't know what to—"

Cynnie felt for the panicking child. "It's okay, nothing that can't be fixed. Why don't you tell me *why* you're climbing in my window?"

The girl's face burned with shame and embarrassment, but she kept her head up defiantly. "It was a dare. There's this old story about a witch that lives here and eats children. One kid gets dared to sneak in and take something that belongs to the witch each Halloween. If you do, no one can touch you for a year."

Cynnie's eyes narrowed. "What do you mean 'touch you?'"

"Hit you, or anything. No bullies for a year." The girl bowed her head, ashamed. "I am so sorry ma'am. I didn't know a nice lady lived here. I should've known better."

Little bastards. How desperate have they made this kid?

"Well, you're going to go back out there with something that they won't be able to touch you for a whole decade." Cynnie looked around. A satisfying grin struck her face. "Here you go," she said as she pulled the witch's hat from the side table and handed it to the girl. "Tell them you took it while I slept."

A look of complete excitement and awe planted itself on the girl's face as she accepted the gift.

"Thank you so much for everything, ma'am. I've got to be going now," the little girl said as she headed towards the living room window. Cynnie stopped her.

"You can use my front door if you'd like."

"Nah. They might be watching me. Wouldn't look right," the girl said as Cynnie rolled her eyes.

"Well, I'm not sending you out with more lacerations from the broken glass. Come on, you can use the bedroom window. It'll go with your story."

Together they slid the bedroom window open, Cynnie staying out of view. The girl swung a leg out the window.

"Wait a minute, kiddo. What's your name? In case we meet again."

The girl grinned. "I'm Cynnie. Cynnie Parker at your service," she declared as she saluted. She then hopped out and disappeared into the woods.

The girl disappeared. The world spun. Something dripped thickly down Cynnie's face. A bright pain rammed into her head like an ice pick. She placed her hand on the scar to blunt the sharp pain only to feel something wet. A dark red blotch covered her palm. "Cynnie Parker," she muttered.

Memories started flooding back to her in abundance. Fragmented pieces from her past played like movie montages. She remembered being a little girl standing in a hallway with her mother yelling at someone through an open front door.

"We have come to teach her our ways. She must learn now. Her powers will be greater than all of us," voices rang out from outside.

"You leave us alone!" her mother demanded. "She will never be like us! I'll see to that!" Her mother slammed the door and forcefully locked it.

She was sitting at her childhood dinner table, her mother sitting next to her pouring strange things into a glass while looking at a book that sat flat on the table. The page read MEMORY SPELL.

Her mother handed her the glass. "Here you go, baby. This will make you feel better. Those scary women and your nightmares will be all gone. You won't remember any of it. Mama's gonna fix it." The putrid taste slid down her throat. It twisted and burned in her gut. She was going to be sick.

She was going to be sick.

A whisper slid into her ear, cool and soothing, like a hand passing over a fevered brow.

Welcome back, said the voice, a thousand voices, no voice at all. *Welcome home.*

Something pulled her gaze to the portrait of Mildred. But there was no portrait of Mildred.

Above the cold fireplace hung a new painting—a young dark haired woman, green eyes smiling, gazed down at her. A small scar marred her forehead, just above the left eye. The background was black, but discoloration in the paint suggested a shadow, even in darkness.

Cynnie struggled to her feet, as the front door blew open in a blast of chill wind, numberless voices carried on it, whispering incomprehensible words of magic and madness.

Well, thought Cynnie. Here we go.

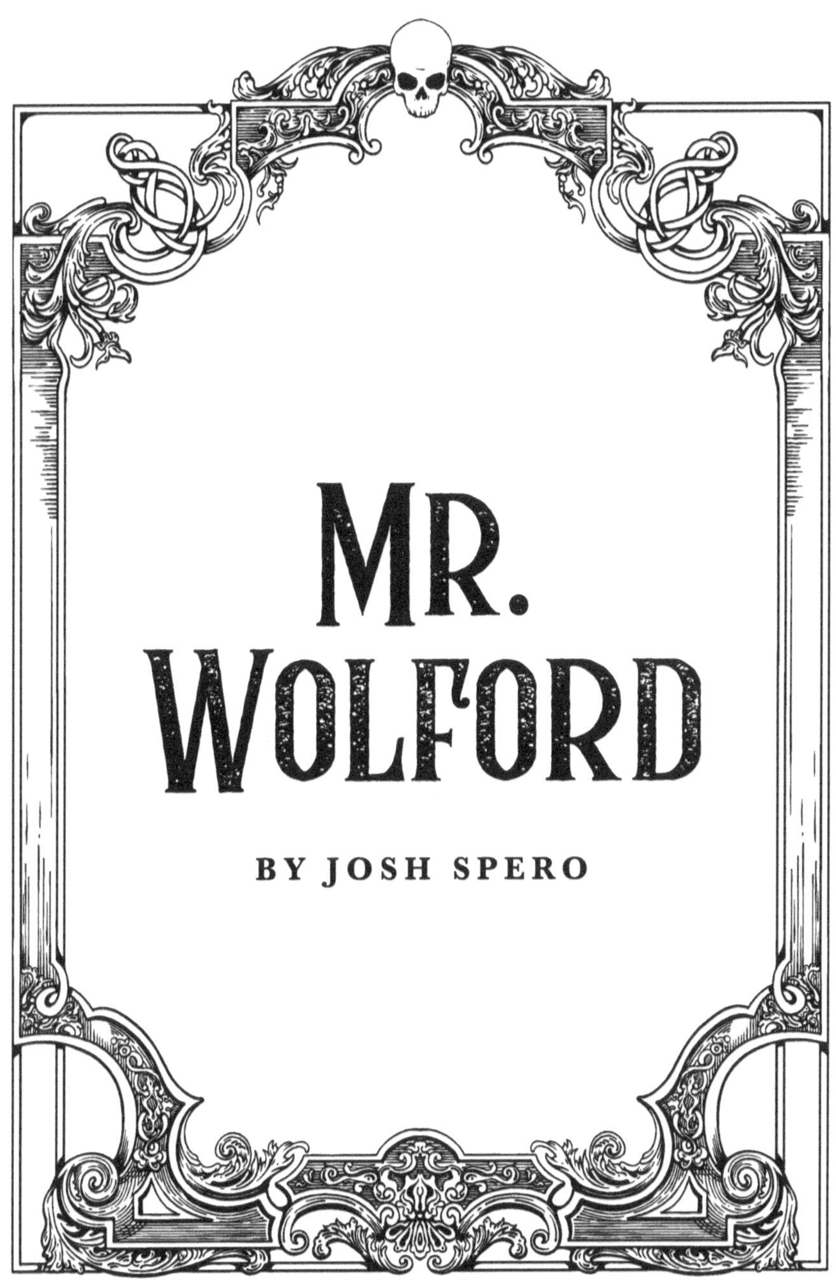

MR. WOLFORD

BY JOSH SPERO

The next door neighbor would always moan,
An elderly man who lived alone.

All through the night we'd hear his voice,
As a neighbor, not the ideal choice.

He'd stay indoors and was hardly seen,
Grumbly, grumpy, sour, and mean.

His house was unkempt, with an overgrown yard,
A wrought iron fence and the windows barred.

Mr. Wolford lived in there,
With a long white beard and long white hair.

We'd never see him come or go,
Only glimpses in a small window.

Yet every night you'd hear him rave,
That would wake the dead right in their grave.

So we called the police to complain,
Impossible, the cops explain.

Instantly we filled with fear,
Mr. Wolford died last year.

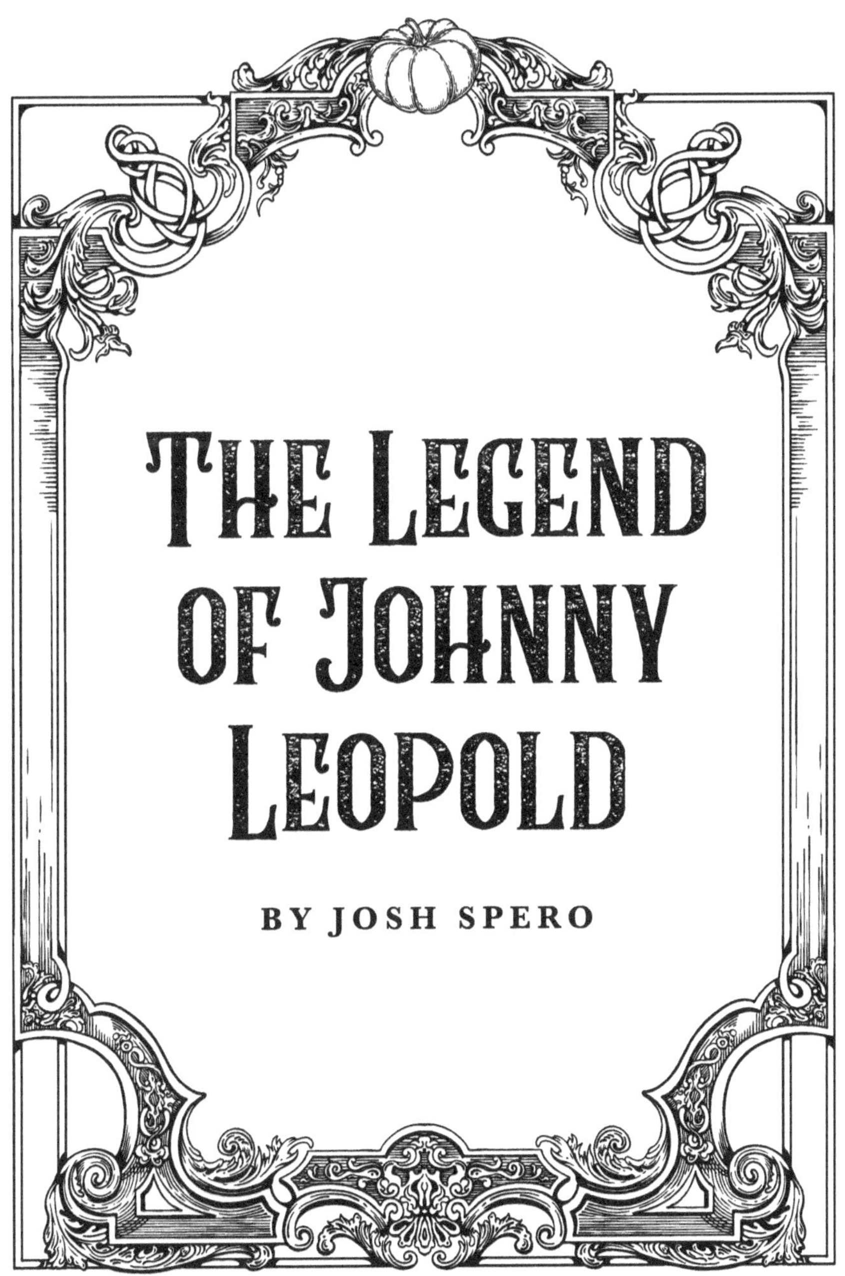

THE LEGEND OF JOHNNY LEOPOLD

BY JOSH SPERO

Where is Johnny Leopold?
This Halloween do what you're told.
Decorate or he'll find you,
Pulling tricks the whole year through.
He'll stay with you until next year,
And every night fill you with fear.
Beware the fate that is foretold,
The curse of Johnny Leopold.

"**C**ome on, you really expect me to believe that mess?" Jack said as he tucked his son Brandon into bed.

"Dad! All the kids swear it's true. Even my teacher says it's real. *My teacher.*"

"So, you're telling me if we don't put up decorations next week, we'll be haunted by a dead kid's ghost for a year?"

"Yeah, and he pulls pranks on you and makes your life miserable and scares you all the time, so you never sleep. Come on, Dad! We have to put stuff up!"

Jack sighed, "We don't have time to get into the spirit. Take a look around, we're still living in boxes and Halloween's less than a week away."

"Yeah, but I know which boxes the Halloween stuff is in!"

"I already checked those—they're labeled wrong. It's the photo albums." Jack sighed at the disappointment in Brandon's face. "We just don't have time to go searching through all the boxes this week, bud. It's just one Halloween. Besides, you won't even be home anyway; you'll be out trick-or-treating and having a good time."

"But what about the ghost?" Brandon asked, his voice small and his eyes wide.

"There's no such thing as ghosts. I Promise. You can still get a costume for school, but no decorating this year. Next year, absolutely. You can go nuts."

"Even one of those giant skeletons?"

Jack sighed and nodded.

Worry swallowed Brandon's face. "Okay. But if this year sucks, it's on you." He pulled his sheets up around his neck and rested his head on his pillow.

His dad gently kissed his forehead. "Goodnight kiddo. Get some rest. You have school tomorrow." The lights went off and the night drifted away.

Brandon had only been attending Harbor Springs Middle School for one week, yet he already had a little posse. Being from a big city like Los Angeles, the other students naturally assigned him cool kid status. The fact that he was a good midfield soccer player didn't hurt his reputation either.

He had already picked up two new best friends: Jimmy Markham, a good-natured nerd, and Jimmy's best friend Mike Temple. Sometimes they would let Will Carnahan tag along with them (even though he was a grade below their own) like a modern day D'Artagnan to their Musketeers.

It was Will who had first brought up the legend.

The four were walking home after school, commiserating over history class, when Will pointed across the street at the Dollar Store. A high schooler was putting out a display of glow-in-the-dark skeletons.

"Mom promised I could get one of those to add to our tree this year."

"Your tree?" asked Brandon.

"Yeah. We have a fancy tree in the front yard, dunno what it's called, but mom lets me hang skeletons from it at Halloween. What do you put up?"

"Nothing this year" said Brandon, glumly. "Dad says we don't have time, there's still a ton of unpacking and stuff."

The other three boys had stopped walking and were looking at each other uneasily.

"We told you about Johnny Leopold, right?"

Brandon shrugged, trying to look chill. "Yeah, but that's just a story. Like the headless horseman or something, like we're reading in English."

Mike shook his head, dark hair obscuring his worried eyes "Nah, my dude, Johnny's real. It really happened. There's a whole thing about it in the town's history museum."

Jimmy rolled his eyes. "It's not a whole thing, it's like one little display thing in a corner." He looked at Brandon, suddenly serious. "But yeah, don't mess with this man, at least get a pumpkin or something."

Brandon frowned. "You guys really believe this stuff?"

The boys looked at each other, then pulled Brandon into a huddle. "Listen," said Mike. "You know our teacher, Ms. Abfell? They were on vacation one year during Halloween, when she was a kid, and when they got back every window in their house was broken. From the *inside.* Nothing else was messed with but there was a ghost costume hanging from the light in the hall. Just like Johnny."

They shivered collectively.

"Anyways," said Jimmy. "Are you guys still coming over for Halloween? Mom said we could make bagel pizzas."

The four walked off into the autumn afternoon, goosebumps up their arms.

The days preceding Halloween grew heavier and heavier with anxiety. Brandon wasn't fully convinced of Leopold's legend, but what if? What if it was real? On the other hand, it was getting easier to be caught up in the distraction that the holiday brought. This town loved their Halloween. He was not prepared for the amount of effort and detail the town put into this holiday and its festivities; and Brandon loved every minute of it. With every passing day, more and more decorations went up and within three days the entire town transformed—store fronts, houses, even the Post Office made an effort for the spooky season. It seemed as though Harbor Springs completely personified the very Spirit of Halloween. Even school lessons were tailored to relevant holiday themes, and the autumn air itself turned to the sweet smell of candy and the promise of thrills.

But in the back of his mind, something stirred uneasily. The more the town decorated, the more Brandon's house stood out like a blight spot on an otherwise perfect apple. The disparity was unsettling.

"Maybe we can at least carve some pumpkins?"

"Sure, the minute we find the box with the kitchen knives in it," his dad muttered through gritted teeth, surrounded by a massacre of cardboard boxes and old newspaper and bits of styrofoam. Brandon knew better than to press the issue.

Halloween finally arrived on a Friday. Brandon woke up and put on his grim reaper costume that his dad had laid out for him the previous night. This was the third year in a row of wearing the same costume; however, nobody in a new town would know that. It was the old familiar smell of that rubber skull mask that almost comforted him and reminded him of the fun of past Halloweens. He put on the same long black cloak and glow-in the dark rubber skeleton hands and headed downstairs for some food.

"Would you stop trying to drink your orange juice through the tiny mouth hole in your mask, Brandon? You're making a mess. Take off the mask and finish your breakfast, will you?" Jack said, struggling not to laugh.

Brandon complied, giggling while he ate. Changing the subject, Jack started, "So let's go over the plan one more time. You get out of school at 12:45 p.m., and you are going over to…"

"Jimmy's house!" Brandon stated, cutting off his dad. "His mom is picking us up. It will be Jimmy, Mike, William and me. We will be eating pizza, trick or treating, and I'll be sleeping over there."

"Okay, just making sure. I'll pick you up in the morning at ten."

From the moment Brandon got dropped off at school his entire day was pleasantly surreal. At school, they did fun and creative activities that were all based on the theme of that day. Every single student was dressed up in every costume he could imagine. His teacher had all types of candy and sweets that they ate while they listened to an old radio play a ghost story in English class. In third period they even watched the 1931 Frankenstein movie. The amount of fun made the school day fly by. Before he knew it, the dismissal bell rang and he ran to meet Jimmy in the front of school. Jimmy was dressed like a Pokémon and hated his costume. He swore his mom dressed him, but Brandon thought Jimmy asked for that costume and it didn't come out like he had hoped. William and Mike arrived soon after in their meeting spot, both wearing the same banana costume.

"I told you I was wearing a banana costume!" shouted William.

"No! You told me to wear a banana costume!" Mike barked back.

"That's okay! I think you're all bananas anyway!" Jimmy chimed in, chuckling while he spoke.

Back and forth they went for a good two minutes bickering like two squirrels fighting over a particularly good branch. Brandon and Jimmy stood by, enjoying the show. They argued right up until Jimmy's mom arrived.

The rest of the evening went off without a hitch. It came and went in a flash. The boys executed all their plans with precision, and it ended up being one of the best nights that Brandon ever had.

Because they had stayed up all night watching horror movies, Brandon was still asleep at ten a.m. when he woke up to the sound of his dad knocking on the front door. Jack was there, right on time with a grave scowl on his face.

"Let's go," Jack said with a foreboding tone.

"What's wrong, dad?" Brandon asked after hopping in the front seat of his dad's car. But Jack remained silent for the whole ride.

As they pulled up to their house, Jack asked, "Did you boys do this? Do you think this is funny?"

Brandon's jaw fell open as they parked in their driveway. He couldn't believe his eyes. "What happened?"

Their entire front yard was covered in at least thirty rolls of toilet paper and broken pumpkins, chunks scattered all over the driveway and porch. Fake blood coated the windows and front door. Worst of all, someone had spray painted a message onto the front lawn—*Johnny is Home.*

Brandon's amazement dissolved into self-preservation after it dawned on him that his dad was glaring at him.

"Oh no! No way! Not us! We were at Jimmy's the entire time!" Brandon cried, a fearful look on his face. It didn't take long for Brandon to suspect the supernatural culprit. "Woah, Dad! Do you think it was…"

"If you say Johnny Leopold's name, you'll sleep outside in the doghouse with Bowser!" Jack said sharply. "If it wasn't you, I'm calling the police. I will not take this lying down."

Brandon looked around again, then nodded slowly. "I think you better call the police."

It took half an hour for the patrol car to arrive, and an older officer met Jack on the front porch.

"How do you do? I'm Chief Deputy Sheriff Michael Gilroy. And wow, what happened here?" The Chief asked, scanning the yard.

"My name is Jack Waller, and I have no idea. I went to bed around midnight, and when I woke up at nine, it was like this."

"Oh, just call me Mikey, everyone does. You mean you didn't hear anything?"

"Not at all. I don't even know who would do such a thing. We're new in this town. We don't have any... I mean, it sounds stupid to say, but we don't have any enemies. We've barely met the neighbors!" Jack threw his arms around in frustration.

"What about Mrs. Waller, did she hear anything?"

Brandon stiffened, and Jack put an arm around him.

"We lost my wife two years ago."

"Oh goodness, I'm so sorry. Well Mr. Waller, we'll file this report and get the team out to investigate. You didn't touch anything, did you?"

"No, not a thing."

"Good, good. I'll get hold of dispatch. Oh, uh, one last question... I don't see any decorations. Did you put some up?"

"*Oh no.* Not you too. I mean no disrespect, but you're a lawman. Are you trying to tell me..."

"What, that Johnny Leopold is real? I mean, respectfully, sir, yes, he was. Terrible tragedy. I knew him and his family very well. But I'm not at all blaming this on a ghost. A ghost who can use a can of spray paint? I will say that townies do love their legends, and some may enjoy an opportunity to prank the newcomers. Probably made you a very clear target, not having anything up." The officer held his hands up in the universal sign of peace as Jack grimaced. "Just an observation. You leave this to me, we'll get right on it."

It wasn't like TV. There was no group of cops standing around drinking coffee and looking at the crime scene. Just Deputy Mikey and a Cadet from the high school armed with an ancient fingerprint kit. After about half an hour, Mikey straightened and sighed.

"Not very promising, I'm afraid, Mr. Waller. But at least you can clean up now."

Ten hours, eight bottles of water, four different outfits, three buckets of sweat, and two showers later, Brandon and Jack finally finished cleaning the gargantuan mess. Brandon was thoroughly convinced that the Leopold curse was now upon them, and Jack was still convinced that some young local hooligans selected their house for the common, but cruel, Halloween prank.

After the cleanup, life went back to normal. School returned to its original, boring norms. William and Mike argued incessantly. Worries about the curse slipped away; weeks rolled on as usual. Brandon relaxed into his new life.

It was November 13 at 2:30 a.m. when Jack woke up to the sounds of hysterical crying and screaming.

"Daddy, Daddy! Help me, Daddy! I fell and I really hurt myself! Help me!" A small voice cried out from another room. In a panic, Jack ripped the sheets off of his body and sprang out of bed like it was on fire. He almost ran through the doors barreling down the hallway. He plowed through Brandon's bedroom door to find him peacefully sleeping in bed. In the ruckus, he woke Brandon.

"Dad? Is everything okay? What's going on?" Brandon asked, worried. "Were you just having a nightmare?"

"No. I don't think so. What happened?"

Brandon felt the panic melt away like warm butter on hot pancakes. "I just…I thought…Nothing; I'll see you in the morning."

It must have been a dream, Jack told himself. He shuffled back to his room and returned to the dream realm in no time. Exactly twenty minutes later he heard the same voice.

"Daddy, Daddy!" the voice said, with a mischievous giggle. Jack woke up this time slightly angry. He sprang up again, only this time he was met by a small figure, holding a Jack-o-lantern over his head, and standing in the hallway door. This time it was Jack that was screaming. At the sight of Jack's fright, the Jack-o'-lantern smiled, then it and the boy burst into flames and faded away in a cloud of smoke. Jack jumped back into bed and pulled the covers over his head as though he was a scared child again. He stayed awake for another two hours shaking like a rattle, when he eventually faded to sleep.

That next morning, Jack was at the breakfast table with a small feast, ready and waiting. Rich smells of eggs with melted cheese, fresh bacon, and cinnamon toast filled the house. Brandon

rarely ate breakfast; however, his stomach started growling like an angry lion. The second his butt hit the chair, his dad started.

"So, tell me more about this Johnny Leopard legend. I need to know what's going on."

"Johnny *Leopold*, Dad. And, I knew it! Did something happen?"

"I'm not sure, okay? It could have just been a nightmare. But I thought I saw… something. I just want to know more."

Brandon pumped his fist in a victorious manner with a huge smile on his face. *"See?* I told you Dad!"

"And now I need you to tell me more."

"Okay, um…there's a poem, we read it in class, I have it in my backpack somewhere. Hang on—"

Brandon rummaged in the baffling mess that is a kid's backpack, pulled out a crumpled half sheet of orange paper, and began to read.

Where is Johnny Leopold?
This Halloween do what you're told.
Decorate or he'll find you,
Pulling tricks the whole year through.
He'll stay with you until next year,
And every night fill you with fear.
Beware of what has been foretold,
The curse of Johnny Leopold.

He smoothed out the paper and put it on the table, then sat down and began to load up a breakfast plate.

"Basically, he was this kid who got grounded for something and didn't get to have Halloween. He climbed up on the roof after his parents went to a party and fell. His ghost costume got caught on the thingy that roses grow on, that looks like a sideways fence?"

"Trellis."

"Yeah, that." Brandon lowered his voice into his best Thurl Ravenscroft impression. "Anyway, the worst part is, his parents didn't realize he was dead until the next morning, because everyone else thought his hanging costumed body was just another decoration. Isn't that *so* scary?"

Jack shifted uneasily. "And that really happened?"

"Yeah. At least that's what everyone tells me. Actually, Mike says there's a display thing about it in the history museum."

"Hmm."

"Did he scare you?"

Jack thought about lying—he wasn't keen on admitting how much last night had upset him. But Brandon was growing up, and it was going to be important for him to learn that even grownups deal with fear.

"Yeah, pretty badly."

"You should get a nightlight," Brandon grinned, stuffing a slice of bacon in his mouth.

"Okay, smart aleck! But really…if it is a ghost.. What are we going to do about it?"

"What can we do? I mean he's a ghost!"

Jack sighed and buttered a slice of cinnamon toast. "I guess we're just going to have to see what happens."

For a week, nothing did. Days passed, and they had a pizza party to celebrate unpacking the last moving box. Mike, Jimmy and William joined them, toasting with plastic cups full of soda.

"You're really one of us now," said Jimmy, grinning.

"Stuck with us for life!" Mike chimed in.

"Or DEATH!" shouted William, covering his face with a piece of pizza and making ghoulish noises. The boys laughed, but Brandon and Jack shared an uncomfortable look.

That following Saturday morning, Halloween was nearly forgotten. Thanksgiving was barreling towards them, and Jack was already making travel plans to go visit his wife's family. He reached up to open a cupboard door for a box of cereal, when the cabinet popped open by itself—and spilled out piles and piles of Halloween candy.

Jack gave a shout, and Brandon went from half asleep to racing down the stairs like a shot. He stopped dead when he saw the kitchen.

Every cabinet and drawer in the entire house popped open, spilling candy like waterfalls. One after another, everything that had a door or a drawer opened on its own with the crinkling sound of waxed paper. *EVERYTHING* was full of candy. Nothing could be opened without hard candy and lollypops spilling onto the floor. Nothing in the entire house was accessible. Piles of candy littered the hallways, like shiny sugar landmines. It was as though Willy Wonka's factory had possessed their house.

Jack and Brandon stared at each other. Brandon had only one thing to say.

"Johnny Leopold."

Jack plopped himself down on the kitchen floor and wedged himself against the refrigerator, with his hands in his hair. He bellowed in frustration. Brandon tried to walk over to his dad, hissing as he stepped on piece after piece. The cracking of hard candy underfoot made them both wince. With one careless move, Brandon stepped on a couple of small jawbreakers and his feet slipped from underneath him. He fell with a hard thud, but instead of giving in to the pain, Brandon started laughing uncontrollably. The laughter spread and, before they knew it, they were both laughing hysterically.

"What do we do?" said Brandon, still stifling a chuckle.

"Clean up."

"Yeah, but *then* what?"

"It's a good question," Jack said, sobering. "I mean, when I think of ghosts, I think of spooky metaphysical figures floating in hallways, you know? But this…" he gestured to the widening mess. "I mean this is more like *Poltergeist.*"

Brandon perked up. "That's it! Dad, what do they do in scary movies when weird crap like this happens? They go research it or look it up in a magic book or something. We should do that!"

Jack nodded and stood, wobbling. "To the museum! Right after we clean this up."

The bleak and obviously neglected sign read HARBOR SPRINGS HISTORY MUSEUM. All Jack could think about was that this museum needed a museum.

"Alright, bud. Let's just be discreet and look into this

ourselves. I don't think we should draw any more attention to ourselves than we already have." Jack instructed.

"Okay. Discreet. Got it." Brandon replied.

The two trudged onward, determined to seek answers. A chime chirped at them as the front door cracked open. They were greeted by a pitchy and crackly voice. "Welcome to the Harbor Springs History Museum. The town was founded in 1880, and we celebrate the founders' achievements here that brought forth our beautiful city. Is there something specific that you boys are looking for?" an old lady recited from behind a counter. She was so small and hunched over that they would not have known that there was someone there if she had not spoken.

Jack thought to himself, *wow, were you one of the original founders?* But he smiled at the lady. "No, ma'am. We are alright…"

"We heard you have a display about Johnny Leopold?" Brandon blurted out, cutting his dad off.

Jack looked at him and threw his hands up.

"Brandon! Discreet!"

"Sorry, dad. Not too sure what that means." Brandon said, refusing to make eye contact with his father. A shrug was enough to break the awkward tension.

"Oh, interesting," the lady responded. "Why the interest in Johnny Leopold? Did you hear something from the townsfolk?"

Brandon spilled the beans—once Jack realized that there was no stopping him, he just stared quietly and shook his head with disappointment. Brandon did not spare a single detail. The little old lady just listened intently saying, "Oh, dear" after everything he said. Brandon finally concluded the drawn-out story.

"That's a darn shame." The lady retorted. "But, there's nothing you can do. Johnny's with you both now. You're just going to have to wait it out and endure. May I recommend sleeping pills? Lots of them. I heard that may help. But, what you are looking for is over there. In that little room is everything on the Johnny Leopold legend."

After thanking the lady, Jack let out a large sigh of frustration. "Alright. Let's get to work."

The room was small and jammed with memorabilia. Pictures, handwritten letters, local newspaper articles, and much more were scattered all over the walls. Hours passed as they scoured everything. They took notice of one specific newspaper article with the headline that read, *Town Devastated after Local Boy Killed in Halloween Tragedy*, dated November 8, 1973. The two looked at each other as goosebumps crawled over both of them simultaneously. Realizing the time, Jack said, "I think it's time for dinner. Want to hit a restaurant and discuss our findings?"

"Absolutely!" Brandon stated.

On their way out, the lady was reading a book to kill time. "Thank you, ma'am, for letting us spend this time here today. Just out of curiosity, were you around here back then? Did you know Johnny?" Jack inquired.

"Well, yes. I was. Oh, I knew him a little. Back then I was a school nurse at his elementary school. I knew him. Not too well, but I knew him." The lady said, as she mentally time-traveled.

Once again, Jack and Brandon looked at each other as their

skin danced. "What was he like?" Brandon asked.

"Here ya go, sweetheart." the old lady said while handing Brandon a pamphlet. It was titled The Story of Johnny Leopold. "Everything you want to know will be in here. That'll be $6.95. Will that be cash or charge?"

New pamphlet in hand, Jack and Brandon decided on burgers at the Rise'n'Dine across the street. They settled into a booth as a waitress with a pretty smile and a scar on her forehead plunked a pair of ice waters in front of them. After they ordered, Jack opened the pamphlet and began reading to Brandon.

Johnny Leopold was a troublesome boy with a heart as big as the Grand Canyon. In the fall of 1973, he started the third grade at Washington Elementary School in Harbor Springs, Michigan. When he arrived at school every morning his entourage would flock to him like flies on fresh dung; the teachers would roll their eyes and breathe a huge preparatory sigh. He was the king of kids and the bane of the adults' world.

The range of his magnetism was not limited to children. Adults found it hard to punish him, no matter how naughty or wicked he was. Perhaps because wildness aside, Johnny was really quite positive and had a zest for life. He merely had a hard time doing what he was told. This kept him in constant trouble. They used to say, "Nothing in life is certain except death, taxes, and Johnny getting detention."

He was relatively dedicated to his learning—but not all school subjects were created equal. This particular year, he detested his history class most. Not only because of the subject (though he hated that too), but more for Mrs. Morganfield, the meanest teacher at WES. She was a cynical, mean-spirited, portly woman, as wide as she was tall, with curly gray-hair and the fashion sense of a brown cardboard box. She was as appealing as a room full of scorpions. Johnny wondered why she never seemed happy to be at school—if anyone was supposed to like school, it was teachers. He guessed Mrs. Morganfield hadn't gotten that memo.

So his zesty personality frequently clashed with hers, landing Johnny in trouble as part of their daily routine. But that was all right. Nothing could dim Johnny's excitement as each school day passed, drawing him nearer and nearer to the dark delights of the spooky season. October was upon them in a flash, and he was in his element.

Halloween was, by far, Johnny's favorite holiday. Every year Uncle Mike would take Johnny and his little brother to the pumpkin patch, which was usually the marker that started the seasonal rituals. The patch was a huge plot of land with hundreds of pumpkins for sale, next to a corn maze they couldn't wait to try. No matter where they stood, the sweet smell of apple cider wafted in the air—along with the accompanying wasps and hornets. In the center of it all was a little farmer's market where they paid for the round orange treasures. Like ruthless pirates, the trio scoured the entire lot searching for the perfect pumpkin to carve. The night would not be complete without buying holiday goodies at the market: homemade pumpkin spiced cookies topped with fresh cinnamon icing, gooey caramel apples oozing down a popsicle stick, and juicy grilled corn on the cob, dunked in melted butter, gloriously salted. The tummy ache that ensued was always worth the indulgence.

The day after their annual trip was just as exciting. It was a day dedicated to carving the pumpkins and decorating his house. He loved to set up the elaborate decorations with his family. The filthier the pumpkin guts were when he carved the pumpkins, the better. There was something about this holiday in particular that captivated Johnny and brought genuine happiness *that no other day brought.*

One golden October day, as Johnny daydreamed about his Halloween plans, Mrs. Morganfield presented a pop quiz to the class. Johnny skimmed through the quiz—with a sinking feeling he began to realize that each passing question grew more and more foreign to him. Taking his pencil, he filled in each set of multiple choice boxes in a pattern: A, B, D, C, then repeated the order until the test was done. He failed the quiz miserably. As punishment, he had to take it home to his parents to get signed; the usual protocol in her class. He brought his quiz home accompanied by a failure notice for the entire class. Johnny walked home a bit slower than usual that particular day, dreading the unknown severity of the situation and its possible repercussions.

He had been right to be afraid. Furious at the news, the last straw of his father's patience vanished and Johnny was banished to his room; his father grounded him for weeks. Johnny protested—that would mean no trip to the pumpkin patch—and no decorating for Halloween. Johnny was devastated. The punishment cut through him like a knife. He begged for mercy, tried to negotiate for two weeks' restriction after Halloween instead of before. He even offered to give up the pumpkin patch if his father would allow him to decorate the house. No matter what persuasion Johnny tried, it was to no avail. His father was done with the school shenanigans and was not budging. For Johnny, Halloween was as good as over.

At least on the weekdays his sentence was broken up by school. But when the weekend arrived, Johnny's room turned into a purgatory. Bored out of his mind, he scrounged up some old comic books that he had already read a dozen times, anything to make the remaining hours fly. It was no use. He couldn't focus. Even Uncle Mike couldn't help him with this one. "Do the crime, serve the time little buddy," Mike said—not ungently—on the phone. "It's not that bad."

But the worst was yet to come. He would be stuck in his room on Halloween night itself.

Johnny sat on his bed, trying to prepare himself to endure the sounds of revelry outside, knowing he was going nowhere fast. Suddenly his heart leapt— there was a knock at his bedroom door! His dad opened it and entered dressed to the nines. Johnny was quite impressed at his father's full-blown tuxedo and Venetian mask but refused to tell him so. Was he here to relent? Was Johnny off the hook? Was he going to get to have a Halloween after all?

"Your mother and I are going to the masquerade ball," his father said. "We hired Jenny to babysit. She knows not to answer the door this evening. We'll be home by midnight at the latest. Behave yourself." Without waiting for a response, his dad left and closed the door behind him. A few minutes later, the car started, and Johnny listened to the sound of the engine growing fainter and fainter, like his hopes for the night.

Usually, Johnny loved it when Jenny would babysit. She reliably fell asleep on the couch around 9:30 if he and Steven kept her up and playing with them long enough. He could do whatever he wanted once he heard the snoring.

Johnny had a plan. Once Jenny fell asleep, he would stuff pillows under his comforter to convince everyone he had zonked out. Then he would sneak up to the attic where the Halloween stuff was kept, climb out the attic window onto the roof, and climb down the drain pipe. It wasn't even twenty-five minutes after his parents had left when he heard the mild jackhammer sounds of snoring. Unable to submit to his sentencing, he made himself the only costume he knew how to, by cutting two eye-holes and a mouth hole in a white sheet he found in the linen closet. Feeling empowered with this costume, Johnny made *his way to the attic, out the window, and onto the roof. Johnny stepped onto a rotted shingle that suddenly tore away under his foot. The shingle slid down the roof, carrying Johnny away with it.*

His mother's rose trellis broke his fall—impaling the boy. He was suspended in the air, lifeless, sheet billowing over him. To passersby, he appeared to be a macabre decoration, one more ghost decoration on the Halloween street. Even his own parents did not realize the truth—they just shook their heads, assuming their son had broken his punishment and decorated the yard. It wasn't until the next morning that Johnny's death was discovered, leaving his family and his whole community devastated.

The pamphlet went on for a few more paragraphs, describing the lasting impact the story had on the community, but Jack was stuck on the passage about Johnny's passing. Across a diner booth from his own son, Jack fought to maintain his composure as tears welled in his eyes. *To lose a son like that*, he thought to himself. *I can't even imagine.* His reverie was broken by a bacon cheeseburger and crispy fries. He smiled at Brandon across the table, winking as he drowned a fry in ketchup. *Well not me. Bring it on, Johnny Leopold, Brandon and I can handle anything together.*

Back home, time started speeding up and the days flew by like race cars on a track. As time elapsed, the pranks kept coming, one after the other. Once, Jack was in the shower washing his hair. While his eyes were closed the water had changed. He opened them to discover that the water had turned blood-red. When he opened his mouth to scream, the water tasted like tropical punch Kool-Aid. Another time, Jack had woken up to the jolting and thrashing of an earthquake. He sat up abruptly to come face to face with

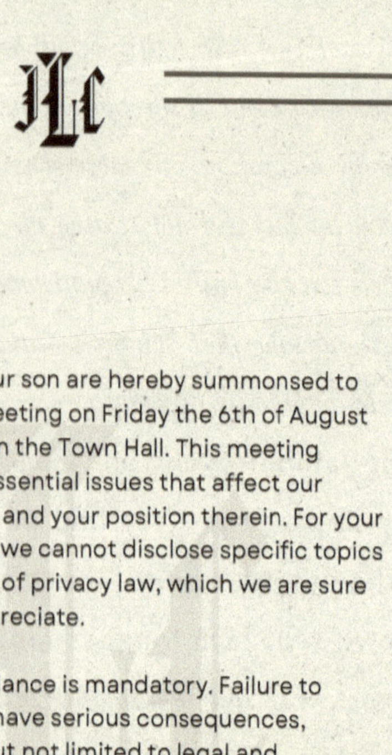

TO :

Mr. Jack Waller
Brandon Waller

Mr. Waller,

You and your son are hereby summonsed to attend a meeting on Friday the 6th of August at 8:00pm in the Town Hall. This meeting concerns essential issues that affect our community and your position therein. For your protection, we cannot disclose specific topics as a matter of privacy law, which we are sure you will appreciate.

Your attendance is mandatory. Failure to attend will have serious consequences, including but not limited to legal and disciplinary actions.

We look forward to your attendance on the 6th.

Regards,

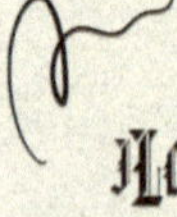

a little figure jumping on his bed wearing a sheet ghost costume. He screamed and quickly turned the light on. As soon as the light illuminated the room the sheet fell to the floor with nothing inside of it. Some of the pranks were tolerable, and some were far worse, but most made sleep scarce. Their nerves were frayed beyond belief. With every creak and crack of the house settling, Jack would spring to attention. It went without saying that this year was the roughest Jack had seen since losing his wife to cancer, and Brandon was just along for the ride.

Nine months of chaos had peeled off the calendar since Halloween, when Jack received a cryptic summons from the Town Hall requesting the presence of Brandon and himself. The letter came with no return address and no formal identification—except the letters JLC, melted into a red seal.

It was Friday evening at eight p.m., the date and time of the summons, and Jack and Brandon arrived at the destination after a silent car ride. Both of them were clueless as to what the nature of this meeting was. All they knew was that the letter said that not showing up was not an option. They both stood in front of the entrance, dressed to the nines, and took a moment to stare at each other. They simultaneously took a deep breath before entering the building.

The lobby of the Town Hall smelled like old mahogany. The building looked as though it hadn't been renovated since 1920. There was a gentleman standing in front of a doorway that welcomed them and instructed them to enter through the door that he was holding open. Jack and Brandon entered an old town committee conference room with hundreds of empty chairs. In the front of the room were five individuals sitting behind desks on an elevated platform, all staring at Jack and Brandon. Behind them were giant gothic-looking banners embroidered with 'JLC' in Old English font. The only person that Jack recognized was the Chief Deputy Sheriff Michael Gilroy.

After a few seconds of awkward silence in a staring war, Jack spoke up, "We're here. What's this about?"

Gilroy spoke. "Mr. Waller. We have several items to address with you this evening, and some of them may be upsetting or hard to understand. I will ask you to remain quiet until we have finished speaking. There will be several questions and concerns that you will have. I assure you, we will address them all." Gilroy pinned them with a fierce glare then continued, "Do you solemnly swear to remain silent until said time?"

Brandon nodded vigorously, Jack with more caution.

"Please get on with it," came Jack's irritated reply.

"We are the Johnny Leopold Council, and we are the governing board that runs Harbor Springs. To my left we have Mayor Philip Roberts, Middle School Principal Sarah Miller, to my right City Manager Frank Patterson, and Financial Director Eric Olson. I tell you this to impress upon you the seriousness of our business here tonight. It is no joking matter."

Jack and Brandon looked at each other, confused. Gilroy continued.

"Mr. Waller, we do things here for a reason, and we treat every offender with the same sternness. We are the people who uphold the legend of Johnny Leopold, honoring his memory with our Halloween tradition—and punishing its avoidance with vengeance. However…it is the feeling of this board that we have gone too far this time. So, on behalf of Harbor Springs, I apologize for all the hardship we put you through; but it is imperative that we instill the importance of this holiday in this town. If we allow one person to not keep the holiday alive, then one will become two, then three, and so on."

Jack shook with rage as the words sank in. "Look—"

Brandon put a restraining hand on his dad's arm. "Hang on dad, let him talk."

Gilroy nodded at Brandon, just at the edge of smiling. "Also, nowadays, kids are not afraid of anything. Giving them a healthy fear of this legend ensures the next generation of avid Halloween fans and thus keeps our traditions alive. This is important for several reasons. For me, it is because of tragedy."

He looked down, and Brandon caught the pitying glances of the other council members. Why were they all suddenly sad?

"Johnny Leopold was a real person. He was my nephew, and he was my favorite person that ever lived. I loved that boy. Enforcing this legend gives his life meaning and allows me to honor him. Which leads me to another important reason we keep this tradition alive. He has now grown into a phenomenon that has caused thousands of tourists from all over the nation to come to our city."

"Our local economy has tripled our calculated projections," Financial Director Olson chimed in. "Tourism dollars, money spent on decorations, people visiting the museum—it's become very important to the health of the community. Just this spring we were able to rebuild part of the hospital wing that came down in that storm last year."

"Not only that," said Principal Miller, "but violent or destructive pranks are basically non-existent at Halloween time. Morale among the kids is high. They love the legend. The story connects them to the past and each other."

"I suppose one of you was the ghost with the spray paint then?" said Jack through gritted teeth.

"I did make sure I only used it on the grass," said the Mayor, sheepishly. "But really…it is such a great unifier in our town. And is that so odd? Most places have their special day or event that they're known for. Ours just happens to be this one."

"And the town is growing, and has been growing steadily since the seventies," Frank commented. "The tourism helps. I don't think it can be entirely a coincidence."

Gilroy nodded at them all. "All this because of my little best friend that loved Halloween. Now, the purpose of this meeting is not to scold you for not decorating; I think we've done quite enough of that. Instead—" he paused meaningfully, leveling his gaze at Brandon. "—we wish to recruit you. You are now *one of us, Mr. Waller.* As an integral part of our community, we want you with us. You must understand, we do not do anything to cause actual physical harm. We do what we feel necessary to enforce the legend. So, what say you? Are you with us?"

A wide array of emotions poured over Jack as if he were

trying to stand under a pounding waterfall. Still trying to process the entire scope of the situation, he stood speechless for about three minutes. "But how? That's breaking and entering. You broke so many laws and—"

"Not exactly, Mr. Waller. We never broke into your house. We were invited." Principal Miller chimed in, cutting Jack off.

"By *who?*" Jack shouted. Suddenly, in his peripheral vision he saw his son raise his hand as if he were in school.

"Sorry, Dad," Brandon said, staring at his own feet.

A look of shock and betrayal swept over his father's face.

"Oh, Brandon."

"Dad, I know you're mad, but these are actually really good people, and they're doing it for a good cause. I believe in what they are doing, and I want to stand with them. Mrs. Miller told me all about it several months ago at school. I believed in it from the beginning, you were the one who rejected the entire thing. Mom died for no reason. I want to make sure this kid died for a reason. Dad, if you love me, you'll understand!" Brandon cried out.

Jack held onto his anger and frustration for about thirty seconds before his heart took the wheel. Brandon was everything to him, and he thought to himself, *What if it was my son that died? Wouldn't I do just as much for Brandon?* Tears started streaming down his face as he said with a quiet wavering voice, "Yes. Yes, we will stand with you."

The council smiled and applauded. Jack held up his hand.

"How did you do all of it?" Jack asked. "How did you guys shoot the projection of the little boy holding the pumpkin that burst into flames? Or the candy that poured out of all the cupboards and drawers?"

The chatter and laughter of the council grew dead silent, and the smiles quickly turned to looks of confusion and concern. A hushed murmur crept over the group. Gilroy sat forward and simply said, "Some of our methods we will not disclose. There has to be some element of mystery left."

"In any case—Mr. Waller, Brandon, welcome to Harbor Springs. Thank you for joining our community and honoring our traditions. We are looking forward to seeing your decorations this Halloween," Mayor Roberts declared with a proper and political tone.

"Thank you for having us," Jack replied, a bit stiffly, putting his arm around his son. Jack and Brandon left the hall and walked quietly back to the car. With his hand on the door handle Jack paused, smirked, and shook his head. He opened the door and hopped in the driver's seat. "Really? You were in on it the whole time?"

"I know! It was so hard keeping it from you."

"Speaking of: you are *so* grounded for a week," Jack blurted.

"Yeah. I figured you would say that," Brandon said, defeated.

"So? What do you think, Bran? Do you even have any ideas for this Halloween?"

"Do I!" Brandon proceeded to explode with endless ideas spewing out of his mouth like an uncontrolled fire hose. Jack knew this was going to be some serious work.

Back at the Town Hall, the council's meeting finally

adjourned. Tired but satisfied, Gilroy returned to the station, then retired to his office, sliding down into his chair. Behind him on the wall hung an old picture—a much younger Michael Gilroy, with two small boys at a pumpkin patch. Mike spun his chair to look at the picture with tears in his eyes.

"Was that you, Johnny? Did you scare Mr. Waller?" Uncle Mike asked.

Suddenly he heard a faint giggling of an eight year old boy.

Mike started laughing behind his tears. "Good one, buddy. We got another one."

IT'S COMING

BY JOSH SPERO

Haunting winds scream through the trees,
Gothic poems heard in the breeze.
Crying souls from just beyond
Await the ferryman to cross the pond.

There's a feeling now, that's in the air:
The promise of a grand affair.
With eerie auras all around,
You sense that something's going down.

With rotting flesh, they now draw near
On each horizon, they appear
They've almost arrived; now it's too late
Once you've been seen, they'll seal your fate.

You fear they crave your flesh, or worse,
They long to place you in a hearse.
With sunken eyes and sharp cheekbones,
They drool and bite, with moans and groans.

They'll circle you, nowhere to run,
Until your nerves become undone.
They're closing in from everywhere,
When all hope fades, it dawns despair.

That's when you take your final breath,
With flowing tears, you wait for death.
You close your eyes against the end,
Knowing soon you will transcend.

You'll join their ranks; it's not that bad,
Although this may hurt just a tad.
But once you turn, your cares will fade,
Just think of the all-new friends you've made.

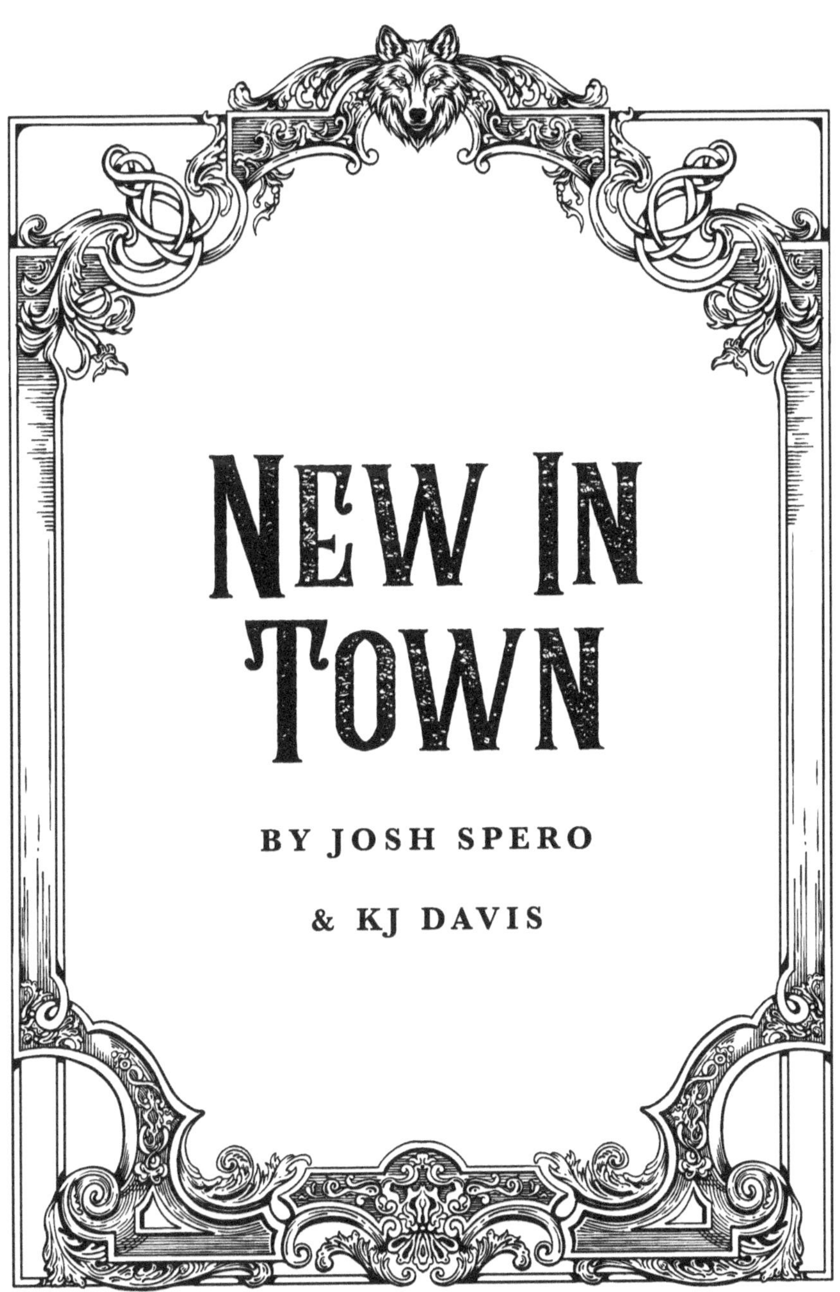

New In Town

BY JOSH SPERO

& KJ DAVIS

What the hell was wrong with you, you idiot! You had no right to sacrifice yourself for me. It should have been me. Why didn't you just run, Tommy? Run away like the others and not look back! Why didn't you just run?

Brian Warner's therapist thinks it might be a liberating exercise if Brian journals briefly to free his mind before school. He takes a deep breath, holds it a few seconds, and exhales as he glances outside at the trees donned in their fall spice shades of paprika, ginger, and chili powder. Below those trees is his new neighborhood of Winston, Virginia, where he's resided for a mere weekend, spent entirely self-imprisoned indoors. He brings his mind back to his room and to the myriad of other journal entries where similar lines of prose, some in bigger bolder print than others, peek from beneath strewn comic books on his floor.

Sure, he thinks, wrinkling his face and mocking the words "free my mind;" *it frees my pen of ink. It frees my papers from their notebook. It even frees my desk and decorates my floor. All it's done for my mind is move it to new space, and now here it all lies in pieces, just like I feel.*

He hears his parents preparing breakfast downstairs, their muffled and polite voices soft in the background of his messy attic loft. He glances outside again and wonders if something grand will ever come along to free *him*—and his desolation.

"Brian!" His mom's voice carries upstairs. "I don't hear any movement up there."

"Sal, leave the boy alone. He'll come when he's ready," his

dad replies.

"Well, will it be this century? He's missing out on all the new moments, Will. The neighbors might think we don't even *have* a son. They've only seen *us*. I doubt his boxes are even unpacked."

"There's not much for him to unpack for. The neighbors didn't even answer their doors both times we visited, but we know they're there. They're avoiding us. It takes time. He'll come around."

Brian slips a plain black tee over his head and shoves his lanky legs into one of three identical pairs of Levi's he owns. Simplicity and comfort always triumph over effort when it comes to presenting himself. Today, he definitely needs comfort for his first day as a sophomore at Kennedy High. He sighs at the unfamiliar face in the mirror, at the darkened expressionless brown eyes, at the sore chapped lips, and the patchy whiskery face that still hasn't made up its mind whether it wants to finish out puberty or stay eternally cherubic. He used to recognize that face—before all the changes.

One more check around the room. He stuffs a pen and pencil in his backpack and scoops the journal off the floor. The last line catches his eye. "Why didn't you just run?" he reads aloud. He rips the page from the binder, shreds it in pieces, and flings them over his shoulder.

Will pours himself some orange juice when Brian emerges for breakfast and points to the plate of toast. "Brian, I thought you were going to make some effort here. What you're wearing says to all the new faces 'stay away.' Can you at least try? This is a second chance, bud."

Brian passes the toast to his dad and looks over his class schedule. "And here I thought it would say, hey, I want to be president of every social club there is because *that's* so me." He slugs down his orange juice before grabbing some toast for himself and scoots his chair from the table. "Have you not lived with me for the past fifteen years? I don't need to be popular. Let them think what they want. Friends can't be part of my life. You know that."

As he rides his bike to school, his dad's words replay in his mind. But his dad is wrong; what happened before always happens again. *This town won't be any different,* he thinks as he locks his bike and pensively ascends the new front steps to his new school. It doesn't have the same smells, the same sounds; it doesn't even have the same chip in the third step from the top like at his other school. He wonders what the day will hold and then stops himself before getting carried away with too many what-ifs.

Calm your anxiety, he thinks. *Just get to the principal's office. It's bound to get better once you're debriefed on their rules and procedures.* But after what seems like twelve hours of listening to Principal Harris blather on about Kennedy High's pride in this, that, and the other, it isn't much better. He's finally dismissed and assumes at last he'll be able to get on with the day.

"Oh, two more things, Brian," the principal says as Brian stands to leave. "The secretary, Ms. Guthry, has a chaperone coming to show you around and I'd like to know—why did you leave the past school? What made your parents move? Appears you've moved often."

Pictures flip in Brian's mind like rigid pages in an old scrapbook; frames of violence, of pain, of darkness. He quickly closes the book. "Oh. Uh, wasn't any big deal. We had issues with neighbors and their pets. But it was—"

"Sylvester! Please come to the office. Office, please, Sylvester," says a crackly older female voice on the intercom, and Brian sighs with relief at the interruption.

"Oh, perfect timing," says Principal Harris. "Sylvester's your chaperone. We'll continue our chat some other time. Enjoy your first day."

Brian forces a toothy smile and closes the door only to come chest to forehead with a chubby, five-foot-nothing, acne-infested student with yellowed sweat stains under his arms and clearly out of breath from wherever he'd traveled.

"I'm Sylvester. You must be Brian," the kid says, pushing his greasy curly hair away from his bespectacled face. "Shall we explore?"

Brian glances to make sure Ms. Guthry has left the office and whispers, "Uh, Brian's still talking to the principal. He'll be another minute." And before Sylvester can speak another wheezy syllable, Brian speeds away to navigate the school on his own.

Before long, hallways resemble other hallways, buildings do the same, and just as he gets a distinct whiff of vanilla and lavender in the air and wonders where the heavenly scent came from, he hears a voice.

"You must be new, not to mention lost," comes a voice from behind him. "Didn't they get you a chaperone?"

"They tried, but he—" Brian turns around to find himself lost in a world of emerald eyes that peek at him behind sandy blonde bangs.

"Let me guess: Sylvester?" The girl grins and flicks her wind-blown hair back over her plaid flannel shoulder. It makes his stomach flutter. "I think they hope he'll step away from the photo lab and develop some actual friends instead of just photos. You can't change a zebra's stripes, am I right?"

Brian opens his mouth to answer but the words stick to the back of his throat, so he just stares awkwardly.

"Bethany," she offers her hand to shake his. "And you are?"

He extends his hand. "Bruin, uh, Brian." *My god, did I just say Bruin?* Her hand is so soft, and she smells as good as she looks in those black Levi's and carpenter boots.

"Okay, Bruin, uh, Brian. I can show you around. Let's go."

Words, you need words, he begs himself. She's cute but stop staring or she'll run away and leave you looking like an idiot in the hall! Be cool! "What makes you think I'm lost? I think I was doing all right. I have science this period."

Bethany peeks at the schedule in his hand. "Hmmm, except this is the Home Ec. hall——unless you're intent on sewing or cooking for the next fourteen weeks, but hey, I'm down with that vibe."

Brian finally relaxes and smiles. "Okay, so maybe I'm lost."

"Then let's get this tour started, shall we?"

They discover they have several of the same classes, so from that day forward they spend time ambling through the same hallways together. Bethany's spirited chatter is answered only by more of Brian's awkwardness, and each day that passes his affinity for her grows more than he expects. He does his best to suffocate the feeling.

On the way to Science one day, Bethany pauses and abruptly asks, "So, level with me, are you depressed or is this what you are, a posse of one?"

Her eyes are a galaxy of stars he wishes he could float inside and live among. With only one hallway left to travel, Brian needs to find a voice. He stalls and grins behind his thoughts. *A posse of one? I wish I wasn't. She deserves more than this, a friend, a companion—not a geeky guy hiding behind a secret I'm dying to share but never can. I want her to know everything, I do! But I can't let her get close to me, I can't!*

"Neither. Well, that is—I don't—I can't—" he sighs. "I suck at being human, I guess."

Bethany snorts and laughs.

Great, he thinks. *She's laughing.*

"I know what you mean," Bethany says. "Sometimes I suck at the human part as well, so I stick to sports. But, hey, the fall dance is coming up. Thought maybe you'd like to—"

Before she finishes, Brian finds a reason to leave the conversation and leave it fast. "I just remembered my locker—I left it, I mean I forgot it—forgot something. Catch up with you in class."

"Brian, wait! Where are you going? The bell is going to ring!"

All the way to his locker, the cover on that scrapbook bursts open again. The pages flick through his mind; pictures of camping in the woods with friends five years prior, of newspaper articles reporting wild animal attacks two counties over—attacks on livestock and people alike. As hesitant as his parents were to let him go, Brian and his friends convinced them it would be fine. They wouldn't be far, they had assured them. There were even rumors the beast had been dealt with. So, they went.

Around midnight, the boys were still wide-wake telling ghost stories by flashlight inside their tent. Tommy had been scaring them all evening, growling and snarling if the air had grown too quiet. He had been Brian's hero since Kindergarten—always the brave jokester. So when they heard a twig snap outside the tent, it made them unsure if they should grin or freeze. When Tommy snickered, it made the others feel like the unsettling sound never happened.

That moment was the lightest Brian remembers feeling. Why couldn't that moment be the one to replay in his head over and over? He shivers as he wishes that had been all that happened. But that was when the brittle echoes of a branch cracked too close to the tent and silenced everyone. A throaty growl that rumbled far longer than it should have made time stand still.

"It was only funny the first time you did it, Tommy," Brian had accused. "Stop it!"

"I swear, it wasn't me. Cross my heart, I didn't—"

Brian rounds the Science building and finds solace in the sight of his locker. The next few minutes of that memory are jagged, as though pieces of his scrapbook are missing and faded. The pictures and images are black and white. He tries to make them stop but they keep playing. Sweat forms on his brow as he recalls the long bellowing howl that pierced their eardrums. He remembers shrieks of panic as all the boys fled from the tent into the dark.

Whatever beast it was that night had been hot on his trail once he'd raced away. He remembers the immense fear he felt when he paused in the woods to frantically scout his exit in the unfamiliar terrain. He is brought back to the fierce sting and the intense pressure that he felt on his right shoulder while standing there, lost in those woods. He remembers that the pain was accompanied by something warm suddenly soaking his shirt.

As he reaches his locker, he trips, and his shoulder slams into the metal door while the memories continue to slam into his mind. His shoulder aches. He grabs it. That same shoulder from back then. He relives those final moments before his consciousness faded into darkness. The last pages flick in his memory; glimpses of Tommy, a branch in his hand, facing the thing in the dark.

"NO! LET HIM GO! Let Brian go!"

Then Tommy was a ragdoll in the beast's drooling mouth as

it carried him away into the woods and everything faded to black.

Brian kicks his locker closed and with it, the memory from his mind. *She was going to ask me to the dance, I know she was. I can't take her. Maybe by ordinary daylight, maybe, but I don't go out in the dark anymore. I'm so stupid. Why did I lie to photo-lab Sylvester? If I'd just let him be my chaperone, I wouldn't have met her.*

He slings his backpack over a shoulder and notices Bethany approaching fast. "What was that back there?" She scowls. "Why do you keep blowing me off?"

The moment makes Brian feel like a kid when his mom had caught him playing video games while he was grounded.

"You-you have to believe me—I—I don't—. Honest, it's a reflex, nothing personal, I swear."

Bethany breathes a few times and the scowl melts into a corner grin. "Then, make it up to me! Don't make me late for Science. And hang out with me tonight." She hesitates before she walks away, then winks and beckons with her head for him to follow.

The waves of dread in his stomach fight over the bigger waves of desire to obey—but obey, he does. "Hang on a sec, how did you find me? I could have been anywhere."

"I used my nose. No, silly. You said you were going to your locker, duh! Doesn't take a brilliant detective."

After school, Brian pedals home with a bad case of Bethany-on-the-brain. On one hand, he can't wait to hang out with her. On the other, what possessed him to change his mind? Those waves of dread in his stomach are now tsunamis. He can't help but feel he's forgetting something, but what?

He dismisses it as nerves and coasts up the driveway. He sits and stares blankly at more new surroundings: another new house, new trees, new smells. His hair is tousled by a cool breeze; it carries the barking of new dogs. He recollects past neighborhoods where beloved pets came up missing some nights, or their body parts were discovered the next day.

His father meets Brian at the gate, whistling and carrying tools. The sound the tools make as they hit the concrete jolts him back to the present.

"Hey, Bri! Good day today?" Bill pries off the old deadbolt to the back door.

"It was all right. I have a date tonight. What are you doing?"

Bill dabs the sweat from his forehead. "Just replacing the deadbolts with some solid carbon steel ones. Keep the good stuff in and the bad stuff out. Nothing personal." He winks at Brian. "Hold the phone; did you say you have a *date tonight?* What happened to 'friends can't be part of your life?' Thought you don't go out at night."

Brian's shoulders slump. Why are parents so good at stating the obvious? "I think it'll be okay if I'm home by sunset. It's Bethany, and I—well—uh—she needs help with Science. I—uh—we wanted to do it over pizza and bowling at Vinnie's."

"Science, eh? Is that what the kids are calling it nowadays?"

Brian grunts and grimaces.

Bill drills the new deadbolt. "Relax. I'm glad you decided to make a friend."

Brian grins. "Well, okay, maybe it isn't so much science as much as bowling she needs help with. Would you drop us off?"

"Mm-hmm. As I suspected. If you work with me to get this done, I'd be happy to drop you both at Vinnie's and pick you up at sunset. But sunset is as far as I'm willing to go. It gives us enough time to get Bethany and you home safely."

"Deal! Thanks, Dad!"

Five o'clock arrives, and Brian is pacing nervously up and down the stairs. Did he remember to put on socks? Yeah, but they're…are there clean ones in his drawer? He climbs back up to his room to check. Half-way down the stairs, he can't remember if he brushed his teeth. He glances up in the mirror while he brushes—why is his shirt so wrinkled? Up and down he climbs until he hears a faint knock on the front door. It's now or never. He leaps down the stairs—his feet barely touch the ground—and opens the door. The glorious aroma of lavender and vanilla greets him first, and then there she stands: a flamboyantly feminine exterior has replaced her tomboy school appearance. Make-up. A dress. How on earth do those two little things transform friendly, comfortable girls into terrifying women? *Perfect*, he thinks. *She's gorgeous. I'm adead man.*

A throat clears, a deep sound, bringing Brain's trip to cloud nine crashing back to the ground. He hadn't registered the bushy-bearded giant behind Bethany.

"Brian, this is my dad, Hank," she says. "Dad, this is Brian."

Brian reaches instinctively to shake Hank's hand but has a hard time not staring at the magnificent scar above his right eye that stretches down to his cheek. "Hello sir. How are you?"

"I'm doing okay young man, doing just fine." Hank's hand fits around Brian's like a catcher's mitt and he pulls Brian close for a whisper. "She's gonna chew you up and spit you out. And if she don't, I will." Hank winks. "Nice to meet ya, Brian. Have her back by eight. I don't want my baby girl out in the dark."

Brian stares wide-eyed and gulps. "N-n-no sir, I don't imagine you do. She'll be home before dark."

A bashful silence fills the back seat of the car as Bill drives the two to Vinnie's; Bethany's new appearance and the memory of

Hank's handshake are still too fresh for Brian to relax. Any words he might say are stuck in his brain like it's been disconnected from his tongue. He seeks Bill's eyes in the rearview mirror and attempts to blink an S.O.S.

Bill clears his throat, "So, Bethany, you chose the right guy to tutor your bowling game. Bri here's a natural. Why, he even—"

"Dad!" Brian exclaims and covers his face.

Bethany smirks. "Oh, is that what you told him? *Bri*? I need tutoring?"

Bill eyes Brian in the rearview again. "Sorry, I meant science. I think. Was it science or bowling?"

"Dad! Oh my god, just drive, okay?" Brian sighs heavily.

When Bethany chuckles and pinches his arm, he knows the bashfulness is over, as is the drive. Bill drops them off at Vinnie's and reminds them he'll pick them up right at sunset.

Brian doesn't realize how hungry he is until they step in the door and the smell of fresh oregano, basil, and baking hot pizza dough fills his nose. They order what they want, find a table by the window, and after the first bite Brian finds some wind for his social sails. Soon, their conversation leaps from topic to topic like frogs to fresh lily pads: where they grew up, what they like best about school, what teachers they can't stand, the music they listen to—the list goes on as does the time.

Bethany swallows her last bite and remarks how pretty the sky is. "When I was a kid, I always enjoyed the clouds growing pinker and pinker as the sun got ready to set. My dad told me it was the sky gnomes' lanterns as they made their way home from the cloud factory." She smiles and stirs her soda with the straw.

Brian watches her fingers and envies the straw they touch. "Nice. Sky gnomes and pink sun—oh no, it's SUNSET!" He stands quickly, fishes in his pocket for some money and throws it to the table, then grabs her hand. "My dad's not here, yet, and your dad's waiting." He pictures Hank's catcher's mitt fist then realizes it's the least of his worries. What happens if he doesn't get her home in time?

"Isn't your house fairly close by?" He asks.

Bethany nods. "I know a short-cut through these woods. C'mon. My dad was serious about chewing you up and spitting you out."

"Woods?" Memories of Tommy flood Brian's mind.

"It's not far. I promise."

Twigs snap beneath their rushing feet, leaves swish and crunch. They put their arms up to shield their faces from low branches as it grows darker and darker. Brian isn't sure if it's past sunset or if it's because they're in the midst of so many trees. They'll be okay as long as it isn't nightfall, he tells himself. He keeps a firm hold of her hand as she leads them into a lighter clearing and relief washes over him that it's not nightfall as he had feared. Then, as they move further into it, he realizes it's not light from the sunset he sees, either, but rather light from the luminous full moon above them.

Full moon. When a long bellowing howl fills his ears, Brian isn't sure if it's from his traumatic memory or actually his own. He covers his face in panic and yells. *"Go! Run!* Run home, Bethany, and don't look *back!"*

But Bethany doesn't run. She falls to her knees, sobbing. Brian fights the power of the full moon to give her more time. *"Bethany! Run!* I can see your house from here, *go!"* He is positive that this is the end of her, just as it was with Tommy, only this time it would be *his* mouth to drag *her* away. What would happen to her?

Why doesn't she run? Why? He feels himself changing. His teeth, nose, and mouth grow bigger and longer, sharp fingernails emerge. The pain is excruciating.

Bethany screams and her sobs burst into strange, almost sinister laughter. It's all so confusing and Brian wonders how afraid she is. He uncovers his face to peek just as Bethany's shirt rips from her hunched back. He sees her fingernails growing just like his are. Then, the limbs of her body shake and stretch.

"What's happening?" Brian shouts as both their bodies grow in girth and coarse hair spikes from beneath their skin.

Finally, silence overtakes the woods. Only two snarls are heard as both teens catch their breath and the overhead brilliance of the moon steals their consciousness. From that moment, all he remembers is that the air is alive with echoes of howling.

#   #   #

Brian startles awake. What had happened? Where is he? *When* is he?

And where is *she?*

His eyes focus. He's in his own bed. He smells like the shampoo his mom always wants him to use. His clothes are nowhere to be seen. His mind is fuzzy, but he knows something happened. *I took Bethany to Vinnie's, she looked amazing, my dad didn't pick us up, hang on, why didn't my dad pick us up?* He pats his pajamas and blankets. *How did I get here? We were in the woods and… why am I so tired?* His mother calls up the stairs.

"Brian! Breakfast! Hurry up or we'll be late for volunteering at the library book sale!"

Book sale? But that wasn't until…

"Mom…is it Sunday?"

"Well yeah, honey, why?"

Two days. He had slept for two days.

On Monday, Brian can't wait for school and to see Bethany. He has a million questions and arrives before anyone else to wait for her on the front steps. When he smells vanilla and lavender on a slight breeze, he squints his eyes and finally sees her.

"Hey, can we talk before class?" he asks.

Bethany grins and tilts her head. "Sure *Bri*, what's up?"

He checks around to see no one else is close enough to hear. "You're a freaking werewolf, that's what's up!"

"You say that like it's a bad thing. You are too. I smelled it on you the moment I met you."

He can't help but stand with his mouth agape. "But, how is it—when were you—why didn't you tell me when I freaked out at the sunset Friday?"

She shrugs. "It was cute, you being so protective and all. Who was I to ruin the moment?"

"Is that why you were laughing? Were you laughing at me? Is this a joke? I could have hurt you!"

Bethany rolls her eyes. "Hurt me? You met my father, right. Didn't you hear him howl just before you changed?"

Brian thinks back to that night. "Hank howled? What are you talking about?"

"Duh! We're all werewolves in Winston." She playfully punches his arm and points her finger at him. "And believe me, I can hold my own, in bowling or otherwise."

"Okay, okay, uh, I believe you." With so many questions still begging to be asked, he feels immensely calm and satisfied with her remarkable statement. Imagine, a town of werewolves! No more reason to hide. No more fear of getting close to people. He looks into Bethany's eyes, beautiful, forest, werewolf eyes that he is confident see him for who he truly is.

He floats on air the rest of the day and pedals home with a fresh vision of everything new around him. The new fences, the new grass, the new dogs barking. Filled with excitement, he glides up the driveway to see his parents unloading the grocery bags from the trunk of the car. He grabs the one his mom is carrying and kisses her cheek.

"Wow! What was that for?" Mom asks.

"Mom, Dad, the whole town is—well, I mean, I think the whole town is—"

"Spit it out, Bri. These bags are heavy," Bill says.

"They're all werewolves!" Brian's face is swallowed by rosy cheeks and smiling eyes. "All werewolves like me!"

"Oh, that," Bill answers. "Yeah! We know. Why do you think we moved here?"

"We needed to keep you safe," his mom says.

Bill walks toward the new door he installed. "These extra bolts weren't just for you, pal." He chuckles. "Oh, and uh, I'm sorry about not picking you up from Vinnie's. Hank said to let you two walk home. He said he'd watch over you. You're in good hands."

Brian can't wait for the next day and the day after that and for full moons to come and go for the rest of his life. He is going to have friends and do all the things that normal teens do. His future is bright and glowing, and he decides to ask Bethany to be his girlfriend right away.

A couple of weeks later, Brian is in History class and wistfully watching Bethany play with her hair three rows away when the teacher announces, "Class, we have a new student today. I'd like you to welcome Tommy Tanner."

Brian springs to his feet. Did he hear correctly? Tommy? His Tommy? But he's been missing—dead. When a tall familiar figure walks into the classroom, Brian calls his name and pushes desks out of the way to get to him. "TOMMY!"

They embrace in a long overdue hug, completely lost in the moment before Brian realizes how quiet the room has fallen and that the eyes of all are glued to them.

Bethany clears her throat and smiles. "Do I have something to worry about here? I'm still your girlfriend, right?"

Brian lets go abruptly and fidgets with his hair. "Oh, uh, I mean, hey, dude!" He slugs Tommy's arm. "It's great to uh, see you again, but we should, uh, you know, catch up later."

"Yeah, yeah, uh, for sure," Tommy replies.

Later that night, Brian sits in his room overlooking the spice colored trees again and watches the sunset. He spies his journal on the floor and opens it to read the entries he's made. "Maybe it did free my mind, after all." He rips his journal into pieces and throws it all in the trash. "But now I feel whole." He smiles. "I'm no longer new in town."

Gone In A Flash

BY JOSH SPERO

Halloween is fun for all,

From Young to Old, Short and Tall.

The night the dead begin to stir,

And roam with monsters all in fur.

Tonight, the Children crowd the streets,

Door to door for tricks or treats.

Living and dead are both the same,

This eerie night of twisted fame.

Faces carved in pumpkins glow,

And light the path for you to go.

The houses all in spooky décor,

Honoring macabre folklore.

When your candy bag gets hard to carry,

Go home to watch a film that's scary.

A slumber party up all night,

Telling stories full of fright.

Eventually you fall asleep,

And back to graves the zombies creep.

You wake, and Halloween is done,

A year remains til the next one.

But you don't have to say adieu,

Spooky Season lives in you.

If you stay eerie in between,

Every day is Halloween.

Well, these adventures are now entered in the Halloween Scrolls of Lore.

It seems Cynnie has a new life ahead of her. Just goes to show that you can't escape your destiny.

Johnny Leopold's legend will appear to live on. His reputation will continue to grow, along with the town, thanks to the JLC and its new members.

Lastly, Brian can finally be happy. Best of luck to his parents, though. I guess parents really will do anything for their children. Even if the situation is a little hairy.

That's all that I have for you this time. I hate goodbyes; unless they're at funerals. So, until the next time...

Stay spooky, my friends.

Jacko

ABOUT THE AUTHOR

Growing up, **Josh Spero** was always fascinated with Halloween and the darker side of things. As a child, he looked forward to the spooky season all year, eagerly awaiting his chance to visit the pumpkin patch, decorate the house with cobwebs and pumpkins, and immerse himself in horror movies and ghost stories. As he grew, his love for all things horror and macabre intensified. His affinity for the season soon became a lifestyle, inspiring him to write and create these spooky tales.

He obtained a Bachelor's Degree in Kinesiology: Exercise Science and a Master's in Applied Exercise Science. Armed with knowledge and imagination, he created this world of twisted tales to entertain and thrill readers of all ages. Through his stories, Josh hopes to capture the spirit of Halloween and inspire others to embrace their love for all things spooky. He lives in Los Angeles with his wife, Robin, and their dog Bailee. He remains enthusiastic about the holiday and is eager to share his spooky tales with others!

SPECIAL GUEST AUTHOR

KJ Davis has excelled as a writer and a poet since middle school. She was an English and Communications major and has a novel in the works.

KJ is married with two sons and four cats and is also a Master Personal Trainer. She spends her time writing, cycling on local bike trails, and training her clients.

INTERIOR ARTIST

TT Hernandez is a multidisciplinary artist, fascinated by the human experience. She has captured the visual narrative for award winning poets, international journalists, lauded composers, and New York Times bestselling authors. Her artwork has been featured internationally at Sundance Film Festival, PBS's POV Docs, Prague & Nottingham International Film Festivals, France Télévisons, One World Media Awards, International Documentary Festival in France, The Boston Globe, M.I.T Museum, The Irish Consulate Boston, and more.

COVER ARTIST

My name is **Aldo Avelar.** As an illustrator I have a passion for art, imagery, and drawing that has shaped my journey. Graduating from California State University of Long Beach in the class of 2020, I began my artistic pursuits during my second year of college. Although I started later than my peers, my love for art drove me to catch up and surpass expectations. Devoting an entire year to drawing every day, both in and out of class, I honed my skills and emerged as one of the top students in my graduating class. Inspirations from legendary artists such as Albrecht Dürer, Michelangelo, and James Jean have motivated me to continually strive for higher standards. While my artistic journey is still ongoing, I remain dedicated to working hard and pushing boundaries to achieve even greater heights.

Castling
Books

If you enjoyed Hall-Lore-Ween try the

MONSTER KID DETECTIVE SQUAD

Book 1: Elsie Frankenstein and the Case of the Disappearing Dogs

Book 2: Sherry Dracula and the Case of the Lunchroom Phantom

Book 3: Rico Gillman and the Case of the See-Through Woman

Find us on amazon.com

castlebridgemedia.com

or ask for us in your favorite bookstore.

(Thank you for your reviews!)

www.ingramcontent.com/pod-product-compliance
Lightning Source LLC
Chambersburg PA
CBHW021558310726
48972CB00003B/850